The bubbly laug
smile settled on British's face. The flickering fire from the room off to the side highlighted the gold strands in her hair. "You don't have to come. I can make up an excuse."

"What?" Donovan feigned again. "I don't want to disappoint your mom. She loves me."

"Good grief." British rolled her eyes. "I'm not going to be able to stomach the two of you flirting."

"Jealous?"

"Please," she quipped. "I am going to bed."

Donovan took a step closer. He liked the way her eyes widened with surprise. She pressed her hand against his chest to stop him.

"Alone," she clarified with a poke in the chest with her index finger.

"Our rooms are right next door to each other," Donovan explained, grabbing hold of her hand. She didn't pull away, just as she hadn't pulled away when he'd almost kissed her on the Ferris wheel. They paused for a moment. Not wanting to waste another second, Donovan dipped his head lower. British tilted her head. And just as he felt the warmth of her breath against his lips, the grandfather clock boldly chimed the midnight hour.

Dear Reader,

My characters Donovan and British both bear scars—
Donovan's may be physical but British's are much
deeper. Who knew a brooding stranger who stands for
everything she's against could help her find balance
and love?

The moment Donovan greeted his future sister-in-law,
Zoe Baldwin, in *The Beauty and the CEO*, I knew he
had a story. Considering the Once Upon a Tiara series
is about life within and after beauty pageants, it was
an adventure writing about a former beauty queen
who is antimakeup and pro girl empowerment.

Raising five boys in middle school and high school,
I've gotten to see firsthand the brilliancy of girls in
STEM programs. If you get a chance, please check out
Tools & Tiaras online and be inspired.

With the bittersweet end in sight for the Kimani
line, I'm getting ready to place the final crown. Stick
around for a glitz-and-glam party in Southwood!

All the best,

Carolyn

Her MISTLETOE BACHELOR

Carolyn Hector

HARLEQUIN® KIMANI™ ROMANCE

Recycling programs
for this product may
not exist in your area.

ISBN-13: 978-1-335-21697-7

Her Mistletoe Bachelor

H HARLEQUIN®
™ www.Harlequin.com

Printed in U.S.A.

Having your story read out loud as a teen by your brother in Julia Child's voice might scare some folks from ever sharing their work. But **Carolyn Hector** rose above her fear. She currently resides in Tallahassee, Florida, where there is never a dull moment. School functions, politics, football, Southern charm and sizzling heat help fuel her knack for putting a romantic spin on everything she comes across. Find out what she's up to on Twitter, @Carolyn32303.

Books by Carolyn Hector

Harlequin Kimani Romance

The Magic of Mistletoe
The Bachelor and the Beauty Queen
His Southern Sweetheart
The Beauty and the CEO
A Tiara Under the Tree
Tempting the Beauty Queen

Visit the Author Profile page
at Harlequin.com for more titles.

I would like to take a moment to dedicate this book to the people near—and far from—me who have lost loved ones. My cousin Jacqui lost her husband, who was her childhood sweetheart. My son's favorite math teacher lost her husband, her college sweetheart. My Shoop Shoop Diva family lost two of our sisters, Betty Williams and Michele Robinson. Through all of this I have been amazed by the way we as family, classmates and friends rally around each other during a time of sorrow.

Acknowledgments

I would like to totally fangirl out and state that the fabulous women of #DestinDivas are my heroes who leave me in awe and inspired after every retreat. And I would like to point out that Miss USA 2017, Kára McCullough, stuck out to me as a shero, proving women can be in STEM and pageants at the same time!

Chapter 1

"Donovan, I can't thank you enough for letting me film this," said Amelia Marlow Reyes, field producer for Multi-Ethnic Television. "Pieces like this are going to drive the website clicks up the charts."

Shrugging, Donovan Ravens scratched the back of his head. As CFO of the globally successful Ravens Cosmetics in Miami, he understood why people were interested in the dynasty—the family, though, not him. Donovan ran numbers, approved budgets and attended company functions. These events, it just so happened, took place at fashion shows and photo shoots. With the company celebrating over fifty years in the business, marketing and advertising had changed. This social-media-savvy generation wanted an up-close look at the entire family through their website. It used to be family photos every other year and placed in traditional magazines like *Ebony*, *Essence* and *Jet*. Now the world wanted to meet each member of the family on a daily basis through Instagram, Twitter and reality TV. The updated website for Ravens Cosmetics offered short videos with a candid look into the life of each member of the family. "I guess. There's not much interesting about my life."

Amelia swatted him on the shoulder. She didn't hit as hard as his sisters did, but the blow did sting through the thick blazer of his tan jacket. "Are you kidding me? The world is infatuated with you. You're the mystery bachelor brother."

"All right, Amelia," Donovan chuckled, knowing she was being kind by not calling him a playboy. As much as Donovan resented his celebrity status, he did not let it stop his dating life, and Amelia knew it. "You already got me to agree to this, you don't have to butter me up."

Amelia pretended to be shocked and lifted her left hand to her heart. Her diamond wedding band flashed under the hallway lights. Donovan heard she'd gotten married a while back to a great guy named Nate Reyes. Given the smile she'd sported all day, Donovan would have guessed she was a newlywed. Amelia's large brown eyes stretched wide, her mouth forming a perfect O. "You can't take a compliment, can you?"

"Let's be honest, I'm not the average pretty boy like Marcus or Will." To prove his point about his brothers, Donovan aimed his long index finger toward the scar that ran down his face, from his left eyebrow to his black beard.

Amelia rolled her eyes. "That only adds to your mysteriousness."

"Whatever," Donovan mumbled before handing over the keys to his two-story condo to Amelia's film crew.

A bulky man with a camera strapped to his shoulders entered the foyer. Another crew member, a woman, carrying a long stick with a furry thing at the end—a boom—followed. Amelia filled the delay with chatter about the next step of filming. Some dude named Vickers tried to contradict everything Amelia said, seemingly pissed off she was there.

Donovan shrugged, still not caring what the old man wanted. Amelia was a friend of the family and the only person he'd agreed to work with on this ridiculous spotlight his sisters, Dana and Eva, thought would be good for the company. The plan was for every member registered to the RC website to gain access to the family via day-in-the-life videos of each one of them. The new line of men's lotions and shaving creams needed to be promoted, and what better way for product placement than in the home of a family member who was also an executive at the company?

"It is tedious. I understand. But to pick up seamlessly from earlier, we need to get your full facial expression as you come inside," Amelia explained.

Someone inside his apartment knocked on the door.

"Wait," said Vickers, "your girlfriend is in there, right?"

The term *girlfriend* made him queasy—*flavor of the month*, sure. They'd dated on and off again with no commitment in sight. Tracy needed a place to crash while her apartment was being painted. She knew the camera crew planned to be here this morning but she swore she'd be gone. Since they dated more on than off and he allowed her to stay at his place unsupervised, he shrugged his shoulders, acknowledging the *G* word might be appropriate. "I guess," Donovan mumbled.

"Wouldn't it be nice if you were to propose to her on camera?"

Fusing his brows together, Donovan took a step back. "Hell no. Amelia?"

Amelia wedged herself between the producer and Donovan. "We agreed—no staged surprises," she said to Vickers.

The dark brown–skinned man adjusted the gold-wired glasses on his face. "Think of the ratings."

"Think about me walking away from this project right now," said Donovan. He took a step back but Amelia turned to face him and grabbed him by the front of his pin-striped Oxford shirt.

"You're not going anywhere, Donovan," she said then turned her attention to the other man. "We're not pulling any surprises. Vickers," she snapped. "Didn't you do your research? The women in his life never make it to girlfriend status. He's only been with Tracy for, like, two months or so."

Six weeks, Donovan mentally corrected her. Once more than a month had gone by without Tracy asking for a spot in a fashion show or a photo shoot in a magazine or asking about getting involved in the family business, Donovan had allowed her to spend the night with him there. Typically, after an evening together, he made sure to send a woman in a waiting limousine filled with roses without a promise of a second date. The *D* word. Donovan did not take women out to fancy restaurants but rather met them out and about. He avoided being photographed as well as being seen with the same woman twice. Better to end things with them sooner than later once they realized that they didn't want to be tied down to a scarred monster.

When Donovan first received his permit at sixteen, he made a foolish mistake trying to avoid an object in the road and ended up overturning his car. He was fortunate to walk away alive, but his head hit the driver's side window, shattering the glass, and then his face slammed into the steering wheel, leaving him with a gruesome scar down the left side of his face. Donovan scratched his face and recalled the first time a girl he liked had told him the truth. No one would ever want to wake up to a face like his every day. Once, on a blind date, he'd overheard a woman complain to her friend for setting her up with Scar but then console herself with the idea of getting access to the Ravens fortune if she became pregnant. Donovan knew he'd never trust that a woman would want him for him, not his family's fortune. Knowing he was a Ravens, women still threw themselves at him. Who was he to turn them down?

So maybe women didn't want to see his scarred face every day, but as he got older and more serious about the family business, women aggressively pursued him. Usually they wanted a modeling job at Ravens Cosmetics, an office position or the chance to marry into the family. He was well aware of the fact that being seen with him brought notoriety and other modeling competitors. The way he saw things, it was a win-win situation.

And then came Tracy. They'd met at a fashion show. She'd walked in with her own fan club. She hadn't wanted Donovan for what he could give her and had even turned down the opportunity to participate in this MET reality special. After four weeks of dating, he guessed she sounded like a winner to him. Last Friday when Donovan had flown out to Michigan for business, he'd allowed Tracy the chance to stay at his place alone. The weekend had been the first step in trust… not something worthy of a proposal. If she passed this step, Donovan planned on getting out of the city with her for the upcoming holiday week.

One of the guys who'd entered the condo before him cracked the door open and asked to speak to Amelia.

Vickers pulled Amelia back by the corner of her blazer. "Let's not forget," he warned in a low voice, "I am the on-site producer here. When this assignment is over, you'll go back to Southwood."

Not liking it, Donovan stepped forward and wagged his index finger in warning at the man.

Amelia shrugged off Vickers's touch, stepped back and shook her head at Donovan as the other producer disappeared inside. "I'm sorry about that."

"Why do you put up with him?" Donovan asked. "Does Christopher know how he treats employees?"

Christopher Kelly, his close friend and scion of the Kelly political dynasty of Miami, had opted to invest in the entertainment world with Multi-Ethnic Television, opening his high-rise building to MET and several other successful businesses in Miami. They had bonded over being offspring of famous parents. And Donovan knew Christopher would not appreciate this behavior.

"Leave it alone," said Amelia with a shake of her head.

The door cracked open again. This time a hand reached out with a thumbs-up. Amelia patted Donovan on the back and nodded to the cameraman behind them. "Now, you open your door and the film crew will start rolling from there. We'll edit it later and splice it into a smooth cut."

Still not knowing all the terms, Donovan crossed the threshold of his place. He'd already been told to ignore the camera and just act natural. "Natural" meant he ripped off his monkey suit and strolled around his apartment in his boxer briefs, but this was not that kind of show. Donovan set his keys on the half table by the door and headed up the curved stairway to his bedroom. One cameraman walked backward, filming him from the front. What happened to the other guy who'd come in first? Weren't there a total of three of them?

Thighs burning from taking two steps at a time, Donovan made a mental note never to skip leg day again. Employees of Ravens Cosmetics took advantage of the gym around the corner of the building. He needed to do so again. The door to Donovan's bedroom was slightly ajar. He heard whispers inside. Was Tracy awake? Did the cameramen wake her?

Pushing the door open farther, Donovan's eyes adjusted to the bright sunshine creeping in from the balcony. His foot hit a bottle and then a pile of clothing. He shook his head at the mess his housekeeper was going to have to clean, then let his eyes wander to a hairy leg poking out of the comforter. The movement in the bedroom didn't disturb the sleeping couple in his bed. Tracy rolled over and wrapped her legs around her partner. The fact Tracy slept with another man did not bother Donovan. His disappointment in himself for beginning to think he could trust someone did. The audacity of her bringing this dude to his place: sheer disrespect. Donovan balled up his fists to keep from flipping them off the mattress.

Whelp, so much for those holiday getaway plans, Donovan thought to himself. Relationships were not in his future.

British Carres flipped her agenda page for the next item up for discussion and her heart jolted. Finally! The Southwood School Advisory Council was going to acknowledge the growing need to fund Science, Technology, Engineering and Math for Girls Raised in the South—STEM for GRITS, an after-school program she spearheaded, involving twenty-plus girls attending Southwood Middle School. Her new robotics group received the hand-me-downs from the boys and it was time for a change. The male robotics team monopolized the lab Mondays through Thursdays, giving British's team only one day in the lab for experiments. The local community collected money currently to distribute to the students in need and after they were all taken care of, a nice pot was up for grabs. Since the language arts, social studies and math departments received a bonus a few years ago, the sciences were next in line. As one of the lower level science teachers at Southwood Middle School, British felt like she had to work twice as hard, putting her degree in chemistry and science from Florida A&M University to good use. STEM for GRITS deserved some of the funds available.

The gray tables in the basement of city hall had been set up in a square so that all the committee members of the school board could read each other's faces. This was the biggest challenge of all. She needed to channel her inner beauty queen and learn to compose her face.

Seated across from her was the thorn in her side, the director of the science department. Dr. Cam Beasley was a "good ole boy" who felt the best place for a woman was in the kitchen. The man loved to point out that British had taken a job as the home economics teacher when she'd first started out, further proving her point of the need for the science club for girls. Cam often forgot science was in everything taught in home ec. British had endured the sexism in the field while attending college. She hated the idea that a new batch of budding scientists could be being held back by some lab-coat-wearing, chauvinistic pig.

Whatever, she thought and looked back down at her paperwork before Cam made eye contact and tried to smile. She feared she wouldn't be able to offer a friendly response. British fiddled with a section of the two-page document where the silver staple bound the papers. Her portion of tonight's discussion was the last on the agenda before they took off for the Thanksgiving break. The bonus money would pay for accommodations, travel and supplies if the STEM for GRITS attended the district science fair, where they'd compete against several schools in Southern Georgia.

"You're not going to get anywhere if you're frowning like that."

Looking up, British watched her teacher's aide, Kimber Reyes, pull out the empty black-metal folding chair beside her and take a seat. "Hey, we're just about to start back up."

"Convenient," Kimber said, shaking her head. "I saw Cam run outside to put the top up on his convertible. He's more afraid of getting the car wet than his dreadlock extensions."

As a former beauty queen, British recognized false hair. She never judged anyone for their hair accessories, but Cam tempted her to start. He looked ridiculous with an extra piece of hair covering the spot where his heavy dreads exposed his bald spot. Though British laughed at Kimber's sarcasm, a feeling of dread came over her. Across the square, Cam huddled with the principal and the superintendent.

A feeling of doom washed over British the moment the superintendent, Herbert Locke, greeted Cam with a pat on the back and whispered something in the science director's ear. The two bent over in laughter of the slap-happy-inside-joke kind. Of course these two were buddies. They probably just made arrangements to visit each other's hunting camps, considering deer season was about to kick off. British needed these funds and she had to get the board to recognize it.

"All right, if we can finish up here," the president of the Southwood School Advisory Committee said, clearing her throat. "I am sure we would all like to get home and start cooking for the Thanksgiving holiday before this storm breaks and leaves us high and dry."

As if on cue a crack of lightning lit up the rectangular windows of the conference room. Everyone groaned.

"Excuse me," British said, standing as others began to gather their belongings. "I believe we missed my part of the agenda." She was never one to bite her tongue and she wasn't going to start now.

Someone sighed in annoyance.

Two of the high school teachers plopped their purses back on the table.

"Sorry to take five minutes out of your evening, but this has been put off long enough and now that we have Superintendent Locke here—"

"You're already two minutes into your time, *Home Ec*," Cam interrupted and chuckled.

British's upper lip curled, hearing the nickname; she twisted the pear-shaped diamond engagement ring she still wore on her finger. Bravery ignited, she cleared her throat. "I don't see how laughing about STEM for GRITS is funny." But as she said the words the rest of the advisory board laughed. Heat filled her cheeks, reminding her of the time when she realized she loved science and the science fairs. She'd been so excited the year she was old enough to make an exploding volcano that she practically ran over to join the boys. Her ears still rang from the laughter of the class when the boys told her she could only clean up after them and handed her a broom. None of her girlfriends, friends who didn't grasp the science behind creating their own lip-gloss flavors, wanted to speak up in fear of how the boys would respond. British knew then there needed to be a better support group for girls.

"Why do you think your girls deserve the bonus funding when we already have a legitimate robotics team that can use the funding?" Cam asked, elbowing the superintendent.

"Because the boys on the robotics team are either distracted by the girls or they're not inclusive."

Locke raised his hands in the air. "Which is it?"

Cam spoke first. "Maybe if your girls dressed—"

The women who'd slammed their purses down gasped at the absurdity.

"The trends these days…" Cam sputtered and tried to recover. "Look, when I was growing up, girls had to cover up and wear long skirts. Shirts were damn near turtlenecks. Nowadays they're wearing basically neon signs for boys to look."

"How 'bout you teach your boys to not stare?" British tapped her paperwork with her pink-polished nails. Maybe today was not the greatest day to wear this cotton-candy color. "May we please focus on the agenda?"

And then the weather spoke for her. A loud boom cracked outside on the lawn; the lights flickered and the air went off. Ear-piercing silence filled the room. Once everyone registered what had happened, they began talking at once.

British could feel her funding being pushed to the next meeting. "Before this meeting adjourns, can we please vote to approve who gets the donation from the city? Maybe the Christmas Advisory Council can weigh in on the matter?"

Miss McDonald, the school's librarian and the parliamentarian of the council, banged her gavel at her end of the table and commanded order just as she did in the library.

"What?" British asked. "We're not going to meet next month and, before the year ends, there's a chance my girls can make it to the Four Points STEM contest. It is imperative to nurture young girls at this impressionable age. We need to continue to encourage their creative minds in science and math, as well as everything else. We need more geochemists like Ashanti Johnson, zoologists like Lillian Burwell Lewis and, of course mathematicians like Katherine Johnson. Is the school willing to sponsor both teams?"

As British spoke she recognized the eye-rolls. She was losing her audience. Everyone wanted to get home. They wanted to be with their families. For the first time this year, the schools planned to be closed the entire week of Thanksgiving instead of the last three days of the week, which was fine, British guessed. She tried to avoid her family this time of year.

"Why didn't you put in your request sooner?" the treasurer asked, flipping through a black binder. "I see no notes here."

"Strange." British glared across at Cam. She twisted her wedding ring round her finger for confidence. "I could have sworn I had submitted it at least every other week since the beginning of the semester, once I heard about the extra funding. Actually, I gave it to you again before the school day started."

Cam shrugged his shoulders. "I don't know what you're talking about."

"I handed in another proposal a week ago." British's nails scratched at the top of the table. Kimber patted her on the back, easing her down.

"Last week, when my football player got hurt during practice?" Cam asked and laughed. "I apologize if taking a student to the ER trumped filing your request."

British's eyes narrowed on the director. "I'm ten seconds away from filing a complaint."

The superintendent stood. "I'm sorry, Mrs. Carres, with limited funding, my hands are tied here. Only one program in the school applied for the bonus."

Kimber spoke up. "What about an after-school group?"

The lights flickered once again and gave everyone a glimpse of intrigue on the superintendent's face. "You have an after-school group? I don't recall a budget for one." He looked over at the principal of Southwood Middle School.

"Mrs. Carres uses the recreation center located directly off the school," Principal Terrence advised, beaming. He offered a wink in British's direction.

"All of its members are from the school?" Herbert Locke asked British.

British nodded. "Yes, sir."

"Who funds this project?"

"I do," admitted British. A lump formed in her throat. When her husband, Christian Carres, died five years ago due to complications from a car accident, he'd left her a lump sum of money. There was nothing she'd wanted more than to help the girls of Southwood, Georgia, so she'd poured the money Christian left her into equipment, safety features, you name it.

"Interesting." Herbert stroked the patch of red hair growing on his chin.

"You're not seriously contemplating her request?" Cam squawked.

"If Mrs. Carres turned in her paperwork and you

failed to turn it in—" the superintendent went on "—I don't feel comfortable not supporting them."

"But my robotics team," Cam said through gritted teeth. "We already made plans. I've seen the competition from Black Wolf Creek and Peachville. We've got this in the bag."

"And how do you know?" asked Coach Farmer. He rose from his seat. The hem of his white pullover shirt acted like a hammock for his protruding belly, which lapped the waistband of his red shorts. He spoke in American Sign Language, which he'd initially learned to communicate with the quarterback. For practice and perfection, he always signed now. "Are you spying on the competition?"

Cam sputtered. His bright face reddened. "Competition? What competition?"

Whispers of doubt spread among the committee. British loved to argue her point but if she stood here and let Cam explain himself, she didn't have to say a word.

"So you're not worried about them," baited British, "but you're worried about my girls?"

"Stop trying to make me out to be some sexist, Home Ec."

"Hold on, now," said one of the high school science teachers. "We have a couple of STEM and robotics teams at Southwood High that stepped back for the middle school to receive the funding, but if we're opening the door, we don't mind stepping up to the plate at the competition."

A disgruntled conversation began. All the science teachers, including at the elementary level, wanted a shot to go to Districts.

"All right. All right." Herbert motioned for everyone

to settle down. "I have one pot of money—we can split it evenly or winner takes all."

"Winner takes all," British and Cam chorused.

"Sounds like we have a Southwood competition." Herbert clapped his hands together. "Two weeks from tonight. That will give everyone enough time to enjoy the Thanksgiving break, have time to spend with their families and then get back to the labs and find something interesting to entertain the Christmas Advisory Council. We'll let them decide the winner. Half of the group is made up of organizers for the school drive, and they may just want to have the CAC do this every year if there's leftover funds."

Thunder rumbled outside at his final words. The school district board members gathered their belongings and attempted to file out the double doors in an orderly fashion. British lingered behind the glass doors of city hall, Kimber keeping her company.

"Don't you guys need to get on the road and head for Villa San Juan?"

"Yeah, Nate and Stephen already left with their families," said Kimber. "I wanted to come out and support you."

British linked her arm through the younger girl's. They locked elbows and began walking out the double doors. Rain pelted the brick walkway. "Did you bring your umbrella?"

"Of course not." Kimber laughed. "But I love walking in the rain."

"I can give you a ride, Kimber."

Kimber tugged on British's arm. "Key word being *love*, as in the fact I enjoy it," she giggled.

Cars began leaving the parking lot. Rain fell harder before their wipers could wipe it away. British sighed and glanced at the dark sky. Not even a single star in sight. "You think anyone would notice if I slept here?"

"You can come over and stay at my place tonight," Kimber offered. "I have a nice bottle of wine we can try out."

When British came to Southwood to work as an aide, she did so at Southwood High School, four years after graduating from there herself. She'd been the youngest aide so far and she'd found it hard to gain the respect of the students, until popular Kimber Reyes had spoken up and vouched for her. Five years later she was here with the same girl, who was all grown up. Well, almost.

British shook her head. "No, thanks. I don't like the idea of drinking alcohol with you."

"I am almost twenty-one and it's nonalcoholic."

"Fake wine," British said with a frown. "I can't drink fake wine with you."

"Can't or won't?" asked Kimber. "C'mon, we can go across the street and get drinks. Hot cocoa."

Across the street, the red lights of a sports bar flashed in the evening light. Sprinkles of rain blew through, dampening the front of British's pale pink shirt. The last thing she wanted to do tonight was to spend the evening in a bar with half-drunk men hitting on her because of her suddenly thin wet T-shirt and lacy bra. She missed simpler times when Christian met her during a rainstorm with an umbrella. Funny, she thought with a soft smile, how the memory of him made her feel safe. "No, I'm going to brave the weather."

The committee members had all pulled out of their spots, the twin streetlights brightening the empty parking spaces. Kimber craned her neck. "Where did you park?"

British lifted her hand and pointed adjacent to city

hall. "I have been parked by the rec center all day. I came straight here after everyone left to go home."

Lightning struck across the high school's football field, illuminating the twin field goal posts. How many Friday nights during junior and senior years had she spent watching Southwood High's game-winning field goals take place over there? *Too many to count.* British half smiled and shook the fond memory away.

The rain lifted enough so they didn't have to shout between one other.

"You ought to get going," British urged Kimber. "I'm going to try to make a break for—"

The words died at a loud crack. A clear, sharp, lightning bolt lit the dark sky right over the rec center. A transformer blew, sparks doing their best imitation of Fourth of July fireworks, and two seconds later, regardless of the downpour of rain, a fire broke out.

"Did that seriously just happen?"

Neither of the ladies moved. They both clung to each other. The building went up in smoke, much like British's dreams.

Sunday morning, British found herself seated on a bicycle just outside the gates of the Magnolia Palace hotel. She'd been here before, competing in a few pageants when the roof on Southwood's theater had leaked. There was something to be said about the old structures of her hometown. British inhaled deeply with pride, as if she had a connection with the building.

The fire at the rec center hadn't just ruined an after-school hangout but also displaced a few of the neighbors next to the building, homes of the girls who were part of British's STEM for GRITS.

Ramon Torres, owner of Magnolia Palace, had graciously offered up rooms at the boutique hotel for them to stay until their homes were fixed. The mayor-elect had recently won the hearts of the town but, more important, British's close friend Kenzie Swayne's, too. The two had married last summer.

British understood there was only one guest booked for the Thanksgiving week. More than likely, the man wanted his peace and quiet over the break and having a group of teenagers running through the hallways was not the ideal vacation. British wanted to soften the blow. The phone inside the pocket of her gray hoodie began to ring. British hopped off her bike seat to answer it, her pink fingernail sliding across the screen.

Kimber's face appeared bright and cheerful, as usual. "Hey, my app says you're at my uncle's place."

"That's just creepy."

"Creepy is having to get the girls together in some back alley looking for cans to collect for that STEM steamboat experiment in order to impress the judges," said Kimber. "You're standing outside the door waiting to ring the bell, aren't you?"

"Maybe."

"Uncle Ramon gave you permission to also use the hotel's facilities so the girls can have space to work and concentrate without interruption. You don't have to explain that to the other guest. I've texted you the code to the gate—only guests and employees have the info. The doors lock after midnight until someone is up and unlocks them or, great idea, a person with the code uses it."

"I hear you," British said with a half smile, "but I get what it's like to want to be left alone. I just want to explain to the man, maybe even prepare him."

Kimber huffed. "Whatever."

"He's a paying customer."

"Whoever he is—" Kimber rolled her eyes "—he'll get over it. What did he expect when he came to a hotel?" Someone in the background called her name.

Kimber looked over her shoulder and said something in Spanish. "All right, Brit, I got to get going, but I want to make sure you're okay. I know the place is working with a skeleton crew since there's only one guest booked."

And here British was, about to interrupt this person's day. Forcing a smile onto her face, British smoothed back the stray hairs that had come loose. "Thanks, Kimber. I'll keep you updated."

With that, the call disconnected and British inhaled the fall air. Finally, the rain had stopped. The last of the hurricane season rains brought in the cooler weather. Somewhere off in the distance someone was building a fire. British imagined a group of kids seated around the campfire, fluffy, fat marshmallows dangling from long branches and twigs, taunting the flames. One of the things British hated about living in an apartment. She couldn't randomly make a traditional s'more.

Of course, she could head out to the country, to her parents', for one, but that would end up with everyone fawning all over her. This time of year was difficult. The cooler weather meant hunting season and the memory of losing Christian earlier than she had ever expected. He was born with an enlarged heart, and no one had thought Christian would make it to his first birthday. He'd defied the odds, making it to twenty-three only to have a deer dart out onto County Road 17. British gulped down her bitter sadness. Given Christian's congenital heart problem, the trauma had been too much. He'd survived the accident long enough to make a final joke about the irony and to assure British he loved her.

British cleared her throat and regained her bearings. She needed to secure the place for the girls. The children she and Christian never had the chance to have.

Bound with confidence from Kimber, British punched in the code to the gates and waltzed down the magnolia-lined path toward the old plantation-style home once owned by the Swayne family, now turned into a boutique hotel. Kenzie Swayne's—British's Tiara Squad gal pal—marriage to Ramon Torres right at the end of the summer had brought the home back into the family.

As children, everyone used to hang out here and swim in the lake behind the house. *Ah, the memories,* British thought to herself. The tires of her bicycle crunched on the fallen thick leaves of the magnolias. A wind howled through the tall trees and a shadow formed over the hotel.

"Time to face the dragons," she said to herself. British parked her bike on the bottom step before grabbing the brown wicker basket filled with an assortment of cupcakes from the local bakery responsible for the extra curves on her hips. A couple of fall treats like the Cupcakery's salted caramel pecan, stuffed spice apple, pumpkin swirl latte and the infamous Death-by-Chocolate cupcake always eased loneliness. And British knew that firsthand.

She took a deep breath, headed up the steps and reached for the door handle, but it wouldn't budge. She remembered that the skeleton crew might not be working just yet.

Setting the wicker basket at her feet, British peered through one of the glass panels to the side of the red door as she pressed the doorbell. A chime set off across the polished hardwood floors of the lobby. The check-in station stood empty, the green lamp dark. Then she caught a glimpse of her reflection. She looked a mess in her bunched-up sweatshirt. How was she going to ask some stranger if he would mind her girls staying here during his vacation?

Fingers grasping the hem of the material, she pulled it over her head, but the hoodie locked around the thick ponytail at the back of her head. Groaning, she bent over and gave it a tug, slipping on one of the magnolia leaves scattered on the porch with the last breeze. Her left ankle hit the basket and, to catch herself, she stepped forward and walked straight into the door.

"Sonofabitch," she hissed.

As the door latch clicked from the inside, British's hands locked in their sleeves. The door opened half-way, revealing a square, masculine jawline of a man. Thing was, it wasn't just any man. One jet-black brow arched in wonder while his full lips, surrounded by a close black beard, twisted upward with amusement. The muscle in his biceps twitched and emphasized the definition, making him appear as if a sculpted African god. Chiseled from copper and mahogany wood. The door covered half his face and body, but the exposed parts left her something that hadn't happened in a long time…speechless.

Chapter 2

After a few days of solitude at Magnolia Palace, Donovan welcomed any entertainment, even if it came from a fumbling woman trying to take off her sweatshirt. Donovan bit the inside of his mouth to keep from laughing in her face now that she realized she had an audience—though he hated to admit to being a little disappointed. The silence he'd allowed had given him the chance to admire the curves of her backside. She wore a pair of black canvas shoes and formfitting, light blue jeans. A lot of faith was put into the band that secured her ponytail of thick, curly brown hair. Donovan noticed her doe-like eyes, round, dark and soft. A basket of food sat by her feet and he realized he must be ogling the chef of the hotel.

Since leaving his condo and Miami altogether, Donovan had taken Amelia's suggestion and returned to Southwood, Georgia—by himself. He'd come here last summer to judge a beauty pageant. The original plans were meant to take Tracy away to the boutique hotel off the quiet lake. He'd thought if she'd survived a weekend by herself in his condo, she deserved a private trip. Now Donovan knew better—he'd dropped the girl and kept the reservations.

After escorting the MET crew out of his place, Donovan had cooled his anger downstairs while waiting for Tracy to wake up. It took every ounce of his body not to throw them and the mattress out the window. Was he that much of a pushover for Tracy to sleep with someone else? Was he that less of a man that she needed to bring someone into his bed? The whole thing confused him. She was the first to say she loved him.

Tracy came down, clearly startled to find him home earlier than expected. Donovan let Tracy and her friend leave with the sheets off his bed. The incident with Tracy further proved to Donovan that love was not meant for him. This time alone got him to thinking. Maybe the idea of having someone to love him forever did sound promising, but he hated himself for getting his hopes up. It saddened him to know he'd never have what his sisters and brother had. A family.

Ramon Torres had promised that no one else had booked the boutique hotel for the last two weeks of November. Since it was just going to be him, Donovan had tried to insist Ramon give his staff the week off. No one needed to brave this weather just to accommodate him. But he wasn't going to turn away good food. Not only did this chef have a great behind, she also had impeccable timing. Donovan had just finished the last premade meal she'd packed in the freezer.

Finally adjusted, the chef turned around. Being CFO of a cosmetics conglomerate, Donovan had seen his fair share of beauty. Women threw themselves at him, expecting him to recognize whatever shade of lipstick they wore as one of his company's. Donovan stayed away from the making of the cosmetics part. He even kept his mouth shut when it came to naming their products. But if he had to ever pick a shade or a name for this color, he'd call it *breathtaking*. The chef smiled a wide, toothy grin. The shade of her lips was a mixture of peach and rubies and matched the blush of her cheeks. She didn't belong in the kitchen. She belonged on one of the gold-framed photos hanging on the walls of Ravens Cosmetics. Donovan cleared his throat.

"Hi," she said cheerfully. "Sorry about that."

"No problem." Donovan thanked God for the bass in his voice not failing him, considering the erection now threatening to rip the fabric of his blue mesh shorts, so much so that he thought he'd taken a trip down puberty lane. "Come on in. The kitchen is this way." Donovan opened the door farther and shook his head. "What am I talking about? You know where the kitchen is."

The woman's manicured brows rose but she didn't say anything. Instead she breezed by him, leaving him in the scent of sweet honey. Once inside, Donovan closed the door, his hand still on the crystal knob, preparing himself for the wince most women made when they saw his face.

"The kitchen?" she asked after turning, not batting a long lash but not moving, either. "You expect me to make you something?"

"Well, I know I told Ramon to let the staff go while I'm here. You all don't have to fret over me," said Donovan, "but the premade plates you made were so good and gone as of this morning."

"I think there's been some sort of mistake..." she began.

"My bad." Donovan chuckled out of nervousness. Why was he nervous? "I thought the dishes were for me. I ate them all. And I could eat a horse right about now." A frozen look of horror flashed across her pretty face. "If it makes you uncomfortable, I can go upstairs so you can cook," added Donovan. "I've just been up here for a few days with no one to talk to. I was getting a little stir-crazy."

"Oh." She relaxed her shoulders, giving Donovan a chance to recognize the band moniker on her shirt: New Edition. He'd attended the concert tour named on that shirt, filled out by full breasts. "You're hungry."

"Pardon me?" Donovan's attention snapped back to the walking sexpot. Sure, she'd tried to cover her curves with the shirt and the sweatshirt she'd wrestled with a moment ago, but Donovan recognized her stunning beauty.

"I remember where the kitchen is," she said, inclining her head down the hallway. "C'mon, I don't mind if you want to watch me cook something for you. It will give us a second to talk."

She *did* ask him to follow her. Donovan took full advantage of the view she offered. This time it was the hypnotic sway of her hips. Damn. And he'd told Ramon to send his staff home. Geez, the things he could do with her for a week alone…

"I feel like I haven't been here in forever," she said.

"Well, it's been a few days, I'm guessing," he replied as they entered the large, open space of the kitchen. Donovan waited where the black-and-white tiles of the hallway met the hardwood of the kitchen.

"What are you in the mood for?"

You, he thought. "How about your name?" Donovan asked.

"British," she said, extending her hand.

He narrowed his eyes on her hand. Why had he thought the chef had two first names? Was it because the taxi driver who'd dropped him off at the hotel was named June Bug? The oversize diamond on her left hand, placed on her hip, caught his attention, disappointing him at the same time. So much for his next move, which would have been to kiss the back of her hand. Donovan didn't do married women. "That's an unusual name."

"Well," British replied, "Joan Woodbury, my mother, is a very unusual woman. And you are…?"

"Not an unusual woman," Donovan answered with a half grin, easing into the friendly banter. "I'm Donovan." He left off his last name for some reason. Since British didn't blink at his scar or in recognition of him, he wanted to remain as anonymous as possible while he was here.

"Nice to meet you, Donovan. Now that we have our names straight, what can I get for you?"

"I'm starving. I could eat anything."

British's laugh was light and airy. He liked it. "You're in the country, Donovan. You ought to be careful about saying 'anything.'"

"A little roadkill never hurt anyone," Donovan, affected by her humor, chortled.

"We could skip breaking out the pots and pans and head over to the Roadside Kill Grill." She reached for her sweatshirt but Donovan patted the counter.

"I'm good with a tuna melt."

British winked. "Good to know. That's one of my specialties. But while you're in town you ought to give it a try. Summer barbecues never end in Southwood."

Surely the wink was meant to be teasing. To be safe,

Donovan frowned and shook his head. "I'm good, really."

"Suit yourself," said British. She turned her back to him and headed for the cabinets, opening them one by one, as if she wasn't sure where to find anything.

"Have you always liked to cook?" Donovan asked. He propped his elbows on the counter and watched her search the cabinets for food. "Been doing it long?"

"Oh, all my life," she said. "What about you? Hasn't anyone taught you how to cook?"

"I *can* cook." Donovan felt the need to clarify when she stopped to gather a can of tuna, a jar of relish and a loaf of bread. She used her foot to kick the cabinet door closed and gave him a questioning look. "This just isn't my kitchen to rumble through, other than the microwave for all the meals you left me, which were delicious, by the way," he added.

As if she didn't know how to take a compliment, British pressed her lips together and inhaled deeply. Her large doe-like eyes briefly roamed to the chandelier before returning to meet his gaze. "Well, um…"

"Besides," Donovan went on, not wanting to embarrass her, "I know how chefs are about having other people in their kitchens. I didn't want to step on your toes."

"This is very true."

After she found the right size bowl, British's lovely hands stirred her ingredients together. She wore a pale pink polish on her nails, which were chipped, and she didn't bother once to hide them from him. She was imperfectly perfect and he admired that. Other than standing behind halfway opened doors, there was no way to hide his scar. Maybe he'd give it a try one day. Donovan needed to remind himself that she was someone else's wife.

"With you being a full-time chef," he began, "do you still like to cook for your husband?"

Not looking up, British stopped stirring. Her shoulders rose, chest lifted, and then sagged back down. "My husband passed away a while back."

So young to be a widow. An ache crept through Donovan's rib cage. His brother had recently wed. His parents had been married since the beginning of time. But he'd never known anyone who looked so young to have lost a spouse. "I'm sorry."

"Thanks," British said with a half smile, which exposed her dimples.

"How long were you married?" *Are you prying? You've just met. And why do you feel like some adolescent kid with a crush?* "You don't have to answer me. It's none of my business. I came here for peace and quiet, and here I am." Donovan pressed his lips together. Why was he rambling? He hadn't done so since middle school.

"You're fine, it's been five years since Christian passed away," she murmured. "We were married for three years but we had been together ever since middle school."

Donovan's eyes widened at the idea of being with someone that long. Tracy had been the longest and that was barely six weeks. "Wow." He couldn't remember who he'd taken to his high school prom. Math being his favorite subject, Donovan calculated her age. "You're, like, twenty-three."

"I'm twenty-eight—" she coughed and laughed "—but thanks."

"Country life must suit you." Donovan inclined his head, not realizing until she blushed that he was flirting. When did he flirt? Women flirted with him.

"Is that what you're doing in Southwood, Mr. Donovan? Trying to find the fountain of youth?"

Donovan clutched his heart. "How old do I look?"

British leaned her head to the side and studied him. "Thirty-five."

"Tell me you worked at a carnival," Donovan joked. He touched his chin and wondered if the gray was beginning to show.

"I know." British beamed and curtsied. Sadness disappeared from behind her eyes. "It's a gift I have." She finished the sandwiches and slid them onto a tray and into the broiler. "So is my tuna melt. You're going to be thanking me in a minute or two."

"I can't wait." Donovan rubbed his hands together. When was the last time he'd shared a meal with a woman who didn't want to hit up the latest hot spot?

"But to answer your question, I don't cook full-time. I am a teacher."

"What?" He held his hand in the air. Though she'd said her age, Donovan had a hard time picturing her in a classroom. Okay, maybe kindergarten. "How did you start off?"

"Well—" British inhaled deeply "—if you can believe it, I started out as a home economics teacher."

"They're still around?"

British rolled her eyes. "You'd be amazed at how many need to learn basic life skills."

"Sorry, it's just I remember there being one at my school and she was eighty and smelled like oatmeal cookies."

"I can smell like cookies if you'd like," teased British. And then, as if remembering her manners, she covered her mouth. Her eyes widened in shock, then she blinked, fanning her long lashes. "I can't believe I said that. I promise I'm not some flake."

"Of course not," Donovan said. "Most people I know get trapped by their own sweatshirts."

British tried not to laugh but did so with a crimson tint spreading across her cheeks. She moved her hands to her hips. "See, and here I thought we were becoming friends."

"We are," replied Donovan. "Fast friends. We even might go out for some roadkill barbecue while I'm in town."

"Speaking of you being in town…" British said as the timer went off. "Hang on a sec."

No gawking or flinching at his scar, lunch, and now a show. Donovan mused over his luck while watching British bend over in front of the stove to retrieve her masterpiece. And a masterpiece it was. Cheddar cheese bubbled on top; presentation was a part of her dish. She glanced around the kitchen and reached for one of the half dozen potted plants sitting in the windowsill. She dropped a leaf on the plate and set it in front of him.

"This looks delicious," he said honestly. His stomach grumbled.

"It's also hot. Give it a minute."

Once the heat from the food subsided, Donovan took a quick bite. His mouth savored every morsel while his stomach cried out for more. He stood from the barstool and began to do a little happy dance. "Damn that's good."

British beamed at his compliment.

"Explain to me what it is you do as a home economics teacher?" Donovan inquired as steam rose from his plate. He craved another bite.

"Okay, so let's be clear here, I only took that job as an

aide and to get my foot in the door with the Southwood school district board system," she explained. "I majored in science education and chemistry. I now mainly focus on science, technology, engineering and math."

Donovan raised his brow but kept chewing. "And you work here at the hotel? I would guess the busy time is the summer around here when teachers are out."

Pressing her full lips together, British visibly pondered. "Of course summers are busy for Magnolia Palace, but this," she said as she waved her hands at the vast space of the kitchen, "really isn't my thing."

"What's your thing, then?"

"I mentor a group of girls."

"Great. In cooking?" Donovan said eagerly. He picked up his sandwich and took another bite.

British shook her head from side to side. The curls of her dark brown ponytail bobbed. Flecks of gold in the strands caught the light. "I have been mentoring a group of young ladies in the STEM world."

"Wait. STEM?"

"STEM for GRITS, to be exact." British cleared her throat. "It is important to make sure women know it is okay to use their brains, not just their faces."

Choking, Donovan set down his sandwich. His left eye squinted, almost making his vision of perfection blurry. *Almost.* "Are you aware of who I am?"

"No."

"Have you ever heard of Ravens Cosmetics?"

While Donovan wasn't a part of the marketing or branding teams, he would suggest they name their next shade of lipstick Mistletoe, because all he wanted to do was kiss her. Something about the bow shape of her puckered lips reminded him of the joy he experienced on Christmas morning. A thought occurred to him, wondering what her mouth would feel like against his.

"I've heard of them," said British. "I'm not completely out of touch with society. Are you one of their models?"

The chuckle stemming from the back of his throat turned into a choke. British came around the counter-top and patted him hard on the back.

"You okay?" she asked, sincere concern in her onyx eyes.

Touched, Donovan nodded and ducked out of the way of her next pat. "I'm good. So you said being a teacher is your part-time gig. Is cooking your other?" he asked and lifted his sandwich.

"Okay, I believe it's time I cleared up this misun-derstanding."

A look Donovan was definitely used to crept across her pretty face as British bit the corner of her mouth and avoided eye contact. His lack of trust in women, especially after Tracy, set him on edge. Why had he lost sight for a moment and thought she would be any different? Since she hadn't known who he was a few moments ago, Donovan wondered what her angle was. What did she want from him?

"Why are you in my kitchen?"

Before Donovan glanced around to see whose angry voice came from the arched entry into the kitchen, he watched British's eyes widen in surprise.

"So here's the thing…" British began to confess, her eyes darting between the newcomer and Donovan. A grin spread across her face.

"The thing is—" the other woman began, storm-ing into the kitchen. She reached for the white apron around British's waist. "I am *Chef* Jessilyn. I am the chef at Magnolia Palace and I don't know why the hell this woman is in my kitchen."

Donovan sat up in his seat.

"The thing is…" said British. "We had a bit of miscommunication when we first met."

"We met twenty minutes ago," Donovan countered. Irritation and disappointment coursed through his veins.

"I came here because I needed a favor," she began.

"Of course you did." Donovan pushed his plate away. For one brief moment he'd thought she was different.

"Jessilyn!" British exclaimed. "Might I have a word with you in private?"

The newcomer, Jessilyn, jammed her hands onto her hips. She was wearing a pair of overalls rolled at the ankles and a pair of green flip-flops with the same-colored-green tank top under the bib. "Oh, you mean like five years ago, when you were the aide for my teacher who left you in charge of my senior class and I asked you for a moment of time to discuss my grade?"

Donovan watched British's eyes rise as if willing the chef to read her mind. He gathered she didn't, or at least didn't want to, when the chef folded her arms over her chest. The whole scene reminded Donovan of being younger and having his older brother, Marcus, hold information over his head. British was up to something.

"You can't possibly still be mad," said British. "It's not like you failed."

"But I did not graduate with a perfect 4.0."

Not sure if this was a private conversation or not, Donovan decided to leave—with his plate. He headed for the porch and sat on the front swing. Along with accepting he'd be alone for the rest of his life, Donovan figured getting involved at any level with another woman was a good thing to avoid.

In three more bites, the tuna melt disappeared. Besides the bickering inside the kitchen, the rest of the property was quiet. Birds chirped in the afternoon sun. At least it had stopped raining. Someone nearby had a fire going. Donovan didn't think there were any neighbors close to the hotel.

Footsteps neared and squeaked on the black-and-white tiles of the foyer. The door pulled open; Donovan wasn't disappointed to find British standing in front of him.

"I apologize, Mr. Ravens, for misrepresenting myself. When you opened the door I was a bit confused myself. You thought I was the chef and you seemed starving." British nodded her head. "I wanted to help."

Donovan set the plate on the seat beside him and crossed one leg over the other. "You said you had a favor to ask of me. I'm curious, what is it?"

"How much of a fan are you of peace and quiet?" British asked with a half grin. Her heart-shaped face flushed with anxiety, probably from having been caught in a lie.

"Humor me and ask."

"Well, now, that's mighty cocky of you, Mr. Ravens," said British. Both hands went to her hips. The stance put Donovan at an even eye level with Ronnie, Bobby, Ricky, Mike and Ralph of New Edition. The next time the band got together for a concert, Donovan was going to have to tell them how close he'd been to them. Realizing she misread his gaze, British folded her arms across her chest. "I didn't realize you weren't a gentleman," British drawled.

"Not a nice thing to say when you're asking for favors."

British pressed her index finger against the dimple of her right cheek. "Perhaps I was wrong in stating I needed a favor. It is more like a warning."

Amused, Donovan came to his feet. He stood a good foot taller than her. "I don't respond well to threats, British."

"It's not a threat. I came over here to warn you that your peace-and-quiet vacation is about to be disrupted by my GRITS."

"I have no idea what you're talking about," Donovan said, enjoying the way she spoke. Who was this woman? Chef? Teacher? Mad scientist?

"Girls Raised in the South." British added an annoyed sigh. "But I wouldn't expect you to understand the importance of women and science and math."

To the contrary, he knew. His family's company succeeded due to the efforts of women in chemistry and accounting. Great-Grandma Naomi Ravens owed her success to the cosmetic products she'd helped develop, combining natural ingredients with science. For the last fifty years the family has partnered with chemists to create bright quick-drying nail polish, products to keep hair healthy and long-lasting lipsticks.

With her hands on her hips, British took a step backward. Her foot kicked the basket he'd forgotten she'd left on the porch. "You sell makeup." The way she said it made his job sound like a dirty deed.

"I am having a hard time understanding what is wrong with cosmetics."

"Nothing," British said through her gritted, pearly white teeth. She really had an untouched beauty, something he didn't see in the industry. Donovan crossed his arms and listened. "Makeup is fine and all, I just want my girls to realize there's more to life than lip gloss and mascara."

"Okay?" Donovan responded slowly. "Why are you mad at me all of a sudden?"

"Because I know your type."

And before Donovan had a chance to form the thoughts to defend himself, British bounced down the stairs toward a pink bicycle. "Unbelievable."

"So how did it go today?"

Before looking up, British swiped her index finger along the rim of the white paper liner of her sweet potato pecan pie cupcake to savor the rich vanilla frosting oozing on the side. A moan escaped her throat. She loved being a taste tester at the Cupcakery.

"I have no idea how or where to start, Maggie," British said to her friend, who waltzed over with a pink-and-black polka-dot apron draped around her tiny waist. For the life of her, British had no idea, one, how Maggie Swayne stayed so skinny working here and, two, why she was even here at all. The social butterfly flitted from fashion week to fashion week yet for the last month she'd resided here in Southwood, her hometown.

"That bad, huh?" Maggie set her round serving tray on the new bar, recently installed. Maggie propped her elbows on the counter. "Want to tell me about it?"

"Are you like the shrink-bartender?"

"Consider me your friendly cupcake-tender."

"I am good," said British.

"I know I am not Kenzie, but you can talk to me."

More pity, British thought. "Trust me, Maggie, I am perfectly fine."

"If you say so. I just know you came by this morning for cupcakes and here you are now."

"Those were for the guest at Magnolia Palace." British cringed just as the words left her mouth, remembering how the hotel once belonged to the Swaynes.

Maggie picked up a white rag and began wiping the clean counter.

"Don't worry about me," said Maggie with an indifferent shrug. "Once Kenzie and Ramon tied the knot last summer, the house basically returned to the family."

"I am not sure that's exactly how it works," laughed British. "It's still a hotel."

Accepting that, Maggie stopped her cleaning and leaned against the counter, close to British. "So who is the guy renting the room for the month?"

Small-town gossip spread like proverbial wildfire and if Maggie Swayne knew something, it'd only be a matter of time before everyone else did. But if Maggie didn't know by now, perhaps it *was* meant to be a secret. A heated flash of memory struck British like the bolt of lightning she'd felt when she'd first laid eyes on Donovan through the fabric tunnel of her sweatshirt. Now that she was clear of the space around him, British was able to think.

British recalled a time when she loved makeup just as much as the next girl. It wasn't until college when she worked in labs that she realized how it served as a distraction for the other scientists. Men acted as if her perfect lipstick lowered her IQ. After a while she stopped wearing it as much. As a former beauty queen who'd often used cosmetics, she should have known. Ravens Cosmetics sponsored high-title pageants. Last year, one of the brothers had judged the big Southwood Beauty Pageant. And now that she thought of it, it had been Donovan. The family had also come to Southwood for Will Ravens's wedding to makeup artist Zoe Baldwin. The Ravenses and their cosmetics were in every print fashion magazine as well as in ads on the internet. Donovan favored his brothers in photographs, but in person? The scar along the left side of his face gave him a dangerously dashing look. Well—British shivered—the man was larger than life.

"Wow!" Maggie exclaimed. "You just got that totally faraway look women get when they're lusting after someone."

British hadn't realized her mouth hung wide open until she closed it. She shook her head and scoffed, "Oh, that is so not true. Whatever. Be quiet."

"What's going on?"

British's eyes flashed Maggie a warning glare when the French doors to the kitchen opened. Out walked Tiffani Carres, British's sister-in-law. Or was it former sister-in-law? Either way, the last person she wanted to find out about this was Christian's younger sister. Since Tiffani's birth, British had always been in her life. Christian had brought British to the hospital to meet her when they were in grade school. The idea of British getting involved with another man seemed like betrayal.

"Nothing," British quickly said.

"Some man has British blushing."

Tiffani, now twenty-two and grown, smirked mischievously. Her dark brown eyes sparkled under her raised brows. "Anyone we know?"

"Tiffani," British said with a warning shake of her head.

"What?" Tiffani blinked innocently. "Don't tell me you're worried about what I would think?"

"We-ell," British drawled.

With a shake of her head, Tiffani rolled her eyes. "Please. Mommy and I were just talking about this the other day."

As if on cue "Mommy," Vonna Carres, entered through the black-and-white French doors, carrying a cardboard box overflowing with green and red garlands. The only things visible other than her black apron with its pink-and-white trim of polka dots were her hands.

"I hear my name," said Vonna over the box, a gold, sparkled star poking out from the top. Her soothing, melodic voice warmed British's soul.

"British is interested in someone," Tiffani announced.

British cut her eyes to Maggie, willing her to understand the thankless, sarcastic smile she flashed. She missed Christian deeply. She still wore her wedding ring to secure his memory. British missed everything about him, from their silly fights to their deep philosophical conversations over '80s vs. '90s music. British accepted she'd never remarry and had never come close to falling in love since. But she missed the company of the opposite sex, still not something her in-laws needed to know. The last thing she wanted to do was let Christian's family think British had betrayed their son's memory by fawning over some random stranger.

While British dated here and there, she never discussed seeing anyone else with her in-laws. Since she wasn't looking to get married, she didn't see the need to bring her dates around her family. Not one of the men she'd been out with had been special enough. No one could make British consider physical contact. But she had to admit, besides a good conversation over dinner every once in a while, the touch of a man's hands might be nice, too. "No one said anything about my being interested in anyone."

"Well, it's about damn time."

Now Maggie smirked at British.

Sliding the box onto the counter, Vonna took a step back and rubbed her hands together. For a half second British thought her mother-in-law was in pain, but the excited smile spreading across her medium-brown skin told her something else. It annoyed British every time someone told her how much Christian had looked like his father. British saw Christian every time she looked at Vonna.

"British, dear." Vonna stepped up to the counter and reached across the marble slate to pat British's hand. "It's been five years. It's about time someone, anyone, catches your attention."

British pulled her arm away, surprised at Vonna's statement. Her shoulders slumped as relief washed over her. "Maggie is speaking out of turn," she explained. "I gave her no information."

"But she did blush," Maggie interjected.

"Why are you even working here?" British half teased. "Don't you have the world to dazzle via social media?"

Maggie snarled and snatched her rag away. "Fine. Whatever. My job here is done."

Once Maggie stepped away to wipe off a silver-topped table in the corner, Vonna raised her left brow and, wordlessly, Tiffani took the box away. "Now that we're alone," Vonna began, "what's going on?"

British glanced to her left and right. The Cupcakery was full but not jam-packed as if there were a new cupcake debut today. There were enough couples at the tabletop and at the bar. When she glanced back up at Vonna, British shook her head. "Please don't tell me you and Tiffani are on the same page about this."

"Sweetheart," Vonna said with a sigh, "I know you've tried your hand at dating."

"Failed dating," British blurted out. "Wait, how'd you know?"

Vonna shrugged her shoulders. "I get my fresh ingredients all around Four Points. People will tell me anything for one of my famous cupcakes when they bring their deliveries here. By the way, what do you think?" She nodded her head at the empty wrapper on British's plate.

"Delicious, as expected."

"It just needs a name, just like you need a man," Vonna continued. "You've been alone too long."

"I'm not alone," British argued. "I have you, Tiff and my family."

"That's not enough."

"I have my students," she boasted. "They keep me pretty busy."

With a skeptical eye, Vonna nodded. "Woman cannot live by the livelihood of children alone."

"Vonna."

Ignoring her, Vonna continued, tapping her short-manicured finger on British's wedding ring. "Do you think Christian would want you sitting around here for this long, pining away for him?"

British wrung her hands together. The rock scraped against her palm, leaving her with an ache. Christian, being diagnosed with hydrotropic cardiomyopathy early on in life, had always made British reassure him she'd move on. His enlarged heart limited their time together. She'd said she would. *When the time was right*.

British's heart swelled at the mention of his name out loud. When he first passed away, her heart would seize and tears would flow. British looked away in shame for not crying right now. Did this mean she was she forgetting him now? "I hear you, Vonna," mumbled British.

"I don't think you do. No one says you have to get married. Maybe a good roll in the hay?"

"Vonna!" British gasped.

"Whatever. But if what Maggie says comes to fruition, I'd like to meet this man at the dance in a few weeks. I promised the school board I'd donate cupcakes for the middle school soiree."

Her mother-in-law pushed away from the counter before British had a chance to deny what Maggie had said. "I promise you, Vonna, if and when I meet the second most perfect guy in the world, I'll introduce him to you."

The silver bells over the front door jingled. British kept her back turned but knew a man must have walked through the door as Maggie swayed against the tabletop with a "Lord Sweet Jesus" sigh. Tiffani cursed when the contents of the box her mother had brought out spilled. Even Vonna straightened and smoothed down the front of her apron.

British smiled and turned to excuse herself when a pink to-go box brushed her wrist. For some unknown reason she apologized then glanced up, only to find herself looking up at none other than Donovan Ravens.

Chapter 3

"Just so you know, your disappearing act is going to cost us a little over a million dollars."

The exaggerated brotherly badgering was not something one wanted to hear the first thing the next morning. It was a Monday. Donovan rubbed a hand across his beard. Since being on this hiatus from work, he'd considered shaving off the damn thing but the double honk of the caravan of cars outside Magnolia Palace reminded him of the visitors rolling into the hotel for the week. What had the hot teacher told him the other day? A couple of schoolgirls and their parents? He sighed and shook his head into the camera of his laptop. On the other end, down in his office in Miami, Donovan's older brother, Marcus, chuckled.

"You don't seem fazed one bit," said Marcus.

"I'm not," Donovan replied. "This time off was requested two weeks ago."

"Vacation suits you. Are you planning on telling me where you are?"

Donovan cocked his head to see around Marcus's big head. "Where's Will?"

Marcus glanced up then back at the screen. "Speak of the devil."

"You guys talking about me again?" Will, their younger brother, said, coming around to Marcus's side of the desk. Both men wore their signature suits, custom tailored at that. "What's up? Where are you?"

"I'm taking care of myself." Donovan dismissed his brothers' curiosity. "What's going on with this alleged million dollars I am costing the company? I am the chief financial officer. I think I'd know if we are in danger."

"We were banking on the announcement for the new face of RC coming this weekend, so we can go ahead and book the production team," explained Marcus. "The crew is now on retainer so they don't take any jobs over the holidays. We had to make a sweet deal in order to do so. Zoe agreed with me."

With Zoe Baldwin, makeup artist extraordinaire on board as the creative director, business had never been better. Profits were through the roof last quarter, and that was despite buying out half of the Ravens cousins for their shares.

"Did Zoe say something?"

"You mean Zoe, my *wife*?" Will clarified his claim by puffing out his chest. Probably the best decision his brother had ever made was marrying Zoe. The two of them together were a powerhouse in the beauty business.

Back before Will had come into the family business, Zoe had been not just a freelance makeup artist, but a good friend of the family business. She'd see Donovan and Marcus on assignment as well as around town at social events. They were friends. Zoe always gave her two Ravens brothers-in-law a hard time about their playboy lifestyle.

Donovan shook his head and huffed in annoyance. "You don't need to remind us every time we talk," he said. "We were at the wedding." The small ceremony was held right here on the same grounds where Donovan was vacationing.

"I just wanted to make sure," Will joked and grinned. "But seriously, she is concerned for you and your relationship with Tracy Blount, after what she heard."

"Are you telling me I have a reputation *now*?" Donovan asked with a smirk. He lifted his coffee mug to his mouth and blew. He could give a crap about the rumor mill. Thanks to the gossip columnists keeping track of Donovan and Tracy's dates, fans were rooting for the supermodel. Hell, he too thought she might have been the one. He admired that she never asked him for anything and liked that Tracy didn't require him to stand as her arm candy at events. But alas, she was just another failed relationship for Donovan, this time caught on camera. When everyone else found out they'd all side with Tracy and pin her as the martyr for putting up with seeing his face every day for six weeks. At least this time there'd be video to explain the breakup. Donovan's ego had taken a blow. What was worse, a woman cheating on you or the fact it happened in his own bed? How humiliated was he going to be? For entertainment purposes he asked anyway. "Wait, what's being said?"

"That you had plans to propose to her," answered Will.

Hot coffee spewed onto the keyboard. "What?"

"That's what I'm saying," said Marcus, smacking

his hand on the arm of his chair. "I wagered a million bucks with Will that there's no way you're thinking about settling down."

"Your money is safe, big bro," Donovan replied flatly.

"Well, when are you coming back?"

"Are bills not being paid?" Donovan asked, emphasizing his sarcasm. He pushed away from the desk and walked backward to the bathroom, where he'd kept his towel from his shower this morning, but it was still wet. He took the shirt off his back and wiped the black keyboard. Will and Marcus groaned. Donovan sneered and winked, proud of the time and effort he put into the gym.

"Put that bird chest away," said Marcus.

"Dear God, man," Will gasped, "your chest is as bare as a baby's bottom."

Donovan flipped them both the middle finger. "Is there a reason for this call or did you just want to bust my chops?"

Marcus leaned back in his chair. "I'm still curious about where you are."

Will leaned close to the monitor and stared beyond Donovan's frame. Donovan pushed the screen to face the ceiling. "Well, if there's nothing else…"

"Wait," said Will. "What's the deal with Tracy?"

Discussing what exactly had transpired in his condo was not something Donovan planned to discuss with his brothers. "What?"

"I'm talking about her being the face of RC next year."

"Not happening," said Donovan, pulling the screen down in time to see Will rake his hand over his face.

"You are aware you're the chief financial officer," reminded Will. "I'm the CEO."

"Do you want to test me, little bro?" Donovan asked his brother with a questioning brow.

"What I want is a fresh new face to reveal at midnight," Will declared without backing down. "One that's not in every music video or perhaps even your bed. Clearly I'm not getting that."

Donovan sighed at his brother. "And why not?"

"Look, I've been courting Tracy's agency for months now. I might be obligated to use her."

The ad campaign was going to kick off Christmas Eve. The makeup for this line had cost millions to make vegan friendly. Donovan hadn't known Will had considered Tracy as the new face, nor did he care. "Find someone else."

"*You* find someone," Will snapped back in annoyance.

Donovan gnashed his teeth together to keep from commenting. He tried to understand the pressure of his younger brother. They, Donovan and his siblings included, helped place him in the position as CEO of Ravens.

"Models are crawling all over this place," said Marcus, the peacemaker. "We can come up with someone."

Will leaned forward to the monitor, pressing his fists on the table. "No. See, this is the problem with you dating the models around here, Donovan. When you get tired of them, it's our job to smooth things over. I'm usually scrambling to find a print ad for your throwaways, but not this time."

"What?" Donovan asked, feeling a headache building. The girls outside his window began to squeal. Now he understood why the teacher had come over here with her tasty bribery basket. No way there'd be peace and quiet with them around.

"I am serious, Donovan," Will said in a clipped tone. "You screwed this up, *you* find the perfect model."

How had Tracy's disrespectful infidelity become his fault? "I'm on vacation," said Donovan with a yawn.

"Not my problem," Will huffed. "If you don't find someone by Christmas, I'm hiring Tracy."

Donovan attempted to weigh his options but couldn't… not with all the hollering. Footsteps echoed down the stairs, followed by parents telling the girls to be quiet and stop disturbing the upstairs guest. Too late.

"Miss B's here!" a girl yelled.

British? Donovan wondered. He stepped away from the desk and strolled over to the open balcony. Downstairs he spotted her, British Carres. She stepped out of a sleek black Accord with gold trim. First came her long legs, encased in a pair of formfitting jeans, a white T-shirt with black writing—BBD, for Bell, Biv, DeVoe, if he wasn't mistaken—knotted at her hip and accentuating her curves. British stood to her full height and with her left hand loosened the bun at the top of her head. Mounds of curls spilled down her neck and over her shoulders. Sunlight caught the natural gold highlights of her tresses.

"Do you hear me, Donovan?" Will yelled. "I am pulling rank on you."

"He's on vacation, Will," said Marcus.

"Oh, and Donovan…" Will called out.

"What?" Donovan growled.

"Make sure the one you pick isn't one you've slept with already."

Donovan leaned against the open door of the balcony and folded his arms across his chest. He was pretty sure he'd found the perfect woman—whether for the ad or for him was yet to be determined.

* * *

British had finally arrived at Magnolia Palace on Monday morning ready for work and perhaps a little rest from constant family calls. With Thanksgiving this week, everyone in British's Woodbury family wanted her to promise to stop by for dinner, as well as the historic Woodbury events after the festive holiday. British purposely left her cell phone in her car and closed the door just as it began ringing again.

Inside the foyer of the hotel, the four competing girls from STEM for GRITS made their way down the steps to greet British. The team voted on their strongest members to start off the competition. Lacey's, Stephanie's, Kathleen's and Natasha's homes had been damaged by the fire at the recreation center. Insurance had covered the roofs but their parents appreciated this time for their girls to be able to concentrate on coming up with ideas for the STEM project.

Thanks to Ramon—and with Kenzie's urging—Southwood had recently resurrected the old post office, turning it into a new recreation center. Unfortunately, because of British's insistence, two teams at Southwood High had booked the new recreation center, also owned by Ramon.

Two of the girls and their families had taken up the offer to stay on the property. The other two girls had come to hang out and plot together today. The last text British had looked at before she'd left her apartment complex indicated that the girls were going to take a tour of the property. British guessed a part of the tour would be a high-speed foot chase. Who said boys were the only ones allowed to be rough?

"No running," British yelled out and accepted the card key from the casually dressed desk clerk. She guessed having more than one guest at the hotel had brought in more staff members for the Thanksgiving week. British offered an apologetic smile and hiked her weekender bag over her shoulder. The simple movement jacked up the short sleeve of her pumpkin-colored sweater on her biceps. The movement caused her to think about the sole guest at Magnolia Palace. Donovan Ravens.

When she'd left the Cupcakery, she'd hoped she had done so without causing any suspicion from her in-laws, Vonna and Tiffani. They, along with Maggie, were smitten and flattered that the handsome stranger had made the trip into town for more cupcakes. If they'd guessed she was the one who had first brought him the cupcakes, they hadn't let on. British found herself glancing upward and held her breath. Was she looking for him? *Dang it, Vonna.* British groaned and pushed her mother-in-law's words out of her mind.

Chef Jessilyn met British in the foyer by the front desk and, a smirk on her face, wiped her hands on a red-and-white-checked washcloth.

"Jessilyn," British began to say as she stared at the red bows tied at the ends of Jessilyn's twin French braids, "it's nice to see you again."

"For the record, I will not be serving you *peach pie*," Jessilyn warned.

The most British could do was sigh in annoyance. Clearly, Jessilyn was never going to get over the grade she'd been assigned. Given the largest peach producers came from the Southwood quad-state area, British's final assignment to her students had been a peach pie. British guessed she should have picked up on Jessilyn's baking talent when she'd turned in a peach cobbler with homemade peach ice cream, but that was not the assignment.

"No one is asking you to," said British. She never knew if Jessilyn, who'd regularly earned a 4.0 since kindergarten, resented having her perfect GPA lowered or if it had anything to do with not respecting British as her authority figure at the time. "Even if you did, I can't go back into the system and change your grade for you."

"Can't or *won't*?" Jessilyn asked with a narrowed glare.

This was going to be a long week. Perhaps she needed to order out for meals. British shook her head and rolled her eyes.

Someone else hollered, "Whoa! Staff crossing here," and then laughed at the chorused apology from the rambunctious girls. Mrs. Fitzhugh appeared at the entrance of the east hallway, dressed casually, like the desk clerk, in a pair of khaki pants and a white pullover shirt. Mrs. Fitzhugh used to work as a seamstress and had seen a lot of British when she'd come into her shop to have a pageant dress altered. Not only was Southwood home to peaches, it also produced several beauty queens.

"I'm sorry, Mrs. Fitzhugh," said British.

The girls appeared at the elderly woman's side. "We need a light signaling someone's in the hallway," Lacey Bonds suggested.

"Or—" British reached out and tugged on the red bill of Lacey's baseball cap "—you could try not running indoors, huh?"

At least Lacey had the common sense to hold her head low as she apologized to Mrs. Fitzhugh.

Jessilyn made her presence known with a scoff.

British inhaled deeply. "I have students who actually want to work, Jessilyn, so if you'll excuse me."

British hiked her bag once more, this time tugging

down her sleeve before stepping onto the circular staircase. If she was going to chase after her students, she needed to set her belongings down.

"Ms. B," Lacey drawled in her rich Southern accent, "we can help you."

The rest of the musketeers—Stephanie, Kathleen and Natasha—came up behind Lacey.

Last summer, the preteen engineering expert Natasha had placed first at robotics camp with her fifth-grade class. She'd been heartbroken when she hadn't qualified to be on the robotics team at Southwood Middle School.

Coding was Kathleen's specialty. She'd coordinated the best back-to-school light show earlier this year in the cafeteria.

As delicate as her name was, Lacey was quite the tomboy and math whiz. She could calculate how much force to put into a soccer ball and where to kick to make it spin. Wholly the opposite of her best friend, Stephanie loved everything girlie. She was their budding chemist. She found a way to counter her parents' rule against not wearing makeup by using cherries to stain her lips.

"Thanks, Lace," British said, not fighting the tug at the handle of the weekend bag. Because she lived in Southwood, British didn't pack a lot of things. Her variety of canvas shoes mainly weighed the most. For a moment she regretted not bringing anything feminine like a cute lacy top and some sandals, just in case she ran into Donovan.

Lacey threw the bag over her shoulder as if it was nothing. "Your room is up here," said Lacey. The energetic girl took two steps at a time and talked over her shoulder. "Mama thought you might want to stay at the other end of the hall, away from us."

"Yeah," Natasha chimed in, making the task a race. Heavy footsteps echoed and rattled the gold-framed portraits hanging from the walls. "Something about us making a lot of noise since Miss Kenzie said the four of us could stay in the same room together. She said there's only one other person over here."

"Wasn't that sweet of her," British cooed with a sarcasm the girls didn't pick up on. "I'm going to have to send her a thank-you note." Kenzie knew what she was doing.

Parents often made beauty pageants awkward and competitive. British was fortunate to start off early with toddler pageants and bonded with the other girls who later became close friends of hers throughout life. They called themselves the Tiara Squad. British served as a bridesmaid to Felicia Ward last summer and attended Kenzie's private ceremony. The other girls in her Tiara Squad had married, and everyone had tried to find a way to get British back into the dating market. If she ever was in the dating market. She'd dated here and there but no one had caught her attention long enough the way Christian had.

With Christian, she loved his patience and understanding. He made her feel like the only woman in the world who mattered. It never mattered if she didn't receive the highly prized title in a beauty pageant; she was always his queen. Christian drove her everywhere and whenever she wanted to speak with other girls at pageants about STEM.

The girls raced down the long hallway toward the private rooms. British knew from past experience when she and her family had come here on the weekends about the some of the rooms connecting. Hopefully in all the renovations Ramon had sealed off the joint bathrooms. The idea of being next door to Donovan caused her heart to skip a beat with anticipation.

"No running," British called out to the girls, who responded with a fit of giggles. The last thing she wanted to do was to disturb Donovan. She wasn't ready to face him again. A flock of butterflies fluttered around in the pit of her stomach. British bit her bottom lip and took a deep breath.

Besides knowing what Donovan did for a living, British had deduced something personal about the man. He'd been in an accident at some point in his life. A serious one. And while the girls were usually polite, they were still children and the X-shaped scar said a lot about the trauma Donovan had faced in his past. British didn't want him to feel bad or to be reminded. Maybe that's why he hid himself away in a hotel in Southwood.

For British, the scar along Donovan's face also told her he'd survived something. In Christian's car accident, his face had hit the steering wheel and the stitches the doctors had tried to put in were in the shape of an X, as well. In the little bit of time Christian had left on earth, he had worried about being seen as a monster and frightening children. It was a ridiculous thought and British had told him so. She would give anything to argue with him over the mark again.

"Ms. B?" Kathleen tapped British's arm.

Snapping out of her daze, British plastered on a smile. "Sorry."

"You were doing that daydreaming my grandma gets," informed Kathleen.

British pouted. "Are you calling me old?"

"Well, compared to us—ouch," Stephanie whined

and pulled her microbraids to the front of her shirt. "No, ma'am."

"Good," said British as she grabbed for her bag and hunched over. "Now let a little old lady get into her room so she can take her afternoon prune juice and nap."

"Tasty," commented a deep voice from the corner of the hallway.

The familiar baritone boomed, making British's heart lurch into her rib cage. She had to clear her throat to release its lodged state. "Donovan."

"So you're my neighbor?" The shadows of the hall-way hid all but his kilowatt smile.

A hard shiver crept down her spine, causing British to jump.

"Sorry," said Donovan, "I didn't mean to scare you." He stepped out from the shadows.

The girls made a collective sigh. Lacey dropped the bag in her hand. Donovan grabbed it before it hit the ground and the other girls' feet.

"I thought I heard a lot of movement going on inside this morning. Here—" he reached for the card key in British's hand "—allow me."

"You're Donovan Ravens," Stephanie finally said.

Donovan glanced over his shoulder, his thick black eyebrows raised. "I am."

"You know who he is?" Lacey asked.

"You don't?" Stephanie countered. "He's only the Chief Financial Officer at Ravens Cosmetics. If you wore a little bit of makeup ever, you might notice."

Donovan opened the hotel room door and allowed the girls in first. British lingered behind and tried to hide her amused smile behind her hand at Donovan's sur-prise. "That's Stephanie," British explained. "Your fu-ture employee in your cosmetic chemistry department."

* * *

Donovan had been around his younger cousins' friends enough to know when they were enamored with one of his brothers. Oddly, these tweens giggled the same way with him. Maybe it was a nervous giggle due to the scar. Each girl avoided making eye contact when British introduced them.

"Thanks for your help, ladies," British said, clearing her throat once they were inside her room.

Taking their cue, the four girls excused themselves but not before eyeballing him up and down. Nothing like a group of teenage girls to make a grown man feel self-conscious. At least his future employee edged her friends out of the room. Or so he thought. Alone, he realized it left just him and British. Given her hand on her hip, the dismissive smirk and raised eyebrow, she was giving him a cue to leave.

"And thanks for bringing my bag in," she said.

Donovan gripped the leather handles and set the weekender on the gold-and-white-striped bench at the end of the mahogany sleigh bed. "What do you have in here, bricks? Oh wait, shoes."

"You're so smart," British said, her eyes crinkling, at the edges. For a moment he thought she might poke her tongue out at him.

The pit of his stomach flopped with the idea of her doing so. Why? Married, widowed or whatever—if she was going to be the face of RC, she was Grade A hands off.

"If you must know, there are shoes in here."

"Since when did Manolo make heavy shoes?" His joke didn't go over well. British narrowed her dark eyes on him. If looks could kill...

She ran her long fingers through her thick, dark,

curly hair. Photographers created lighting with special bulbs and reflections for scenes like this.

"Maybe," she sneered, "you're used to women who pack only expensive high heels, but I'm packing canvas. Converse, to be exact." To prove herself, British yanked open her bag and held up a pink low-top shoe, then a kelly green high-top. She attempted to reach for another but Donovan raised his hands in surrender.

"All right, you win," he said. "I didn't mean to wage war with you."

"What did you plan with me?" British asked.

Dare he say how temptation made his fingers twitch with eagerness to toss her onto the bed and kiss away whatever sadness was hiding behind her eyes?

"Well?" British snapped at him.

"Jesus, lady," Donovan chuckled, "what do you have against me?"

The crinkles in her forehead softened. British blinked her long lashes. "I'm sorry," she sighed. "I don't have anything against you."

"Good."

"Just your company," she added.

An invisible dagger dug into Donovan's chest. "Ouch. May I ask what my company did?"

"Where do I begin?" British scoffed. "You guys hire airhead models that my students then follow and emulate. Before I started teaching Stephanie the importance of women in science, she aspired to be an Instagram model."

Donovan refrained from laughing. He did, however, press his hand to his heart. "Somehow this is my fault?"

"No," British quipped.

Never before had a woman argued with him about

her dislike for the company. Be still, his beating heart. Donovan stopped the argument with a half smile.

"Why are you staring at me with a goofy grin?"

"I think you're perfect," he answered honestly.

A deep red tint spread across British's high cheekbones. She folded her arms over three of the former members of New Edition's faces on the T-shirt. "Do you seriously think your lines would work on getting me to...?" Her words trailed but her eyes roamed to the queen-size bed.

This time Donovan did chuckle. "I think we have our wires crossed."

"Excuse me?" British leaned forward. "You're not trying to get me into bed?"

"I feel like that's one of those loaded questions," Donovan hedged, "where either answer is going to get me in trouble."

British pointed to her door. "Get out."

"Wait," he said, holding his hands up in a pleading defense. "I'm talking about my company. We need a new spokesmodel and I honestly think you'd be perfect."

A few moments went by. A hummingbird pecked at the window. The bells of the grandfather clock downstairs chimed the morning's hour. When British cleared her throat, Donovan was sure she was about to agree. Who wouldn't? Women threw themselves at him for an offer like this.

"Go to hell and get out."

Chapter 4

"All right, girls." British clapped her hands together to get the foursome's attention.

After she'd gotten rid of Donovan and his lecherous offer, British had allowed the girls an hour to run around and do whatever, but now it was time for business.

She closed the white French doors to the library but one of the door handles hit her in the back when it bounced open again. Bright light shone through the solarium porch, which offered a lovely yet distracting view of the lake out back. Sun danced off the ripples in the water and sparkled like diamonds and highlighted books that flanked one another in no particular height or order. Leather-bound classic tales stood next to new romances. Oh, what she would give to spend the afternoon here and put things in order. But she had things to do right now.

Natasha's and Stephanie's eyes were glued to Stephanie's phone. British clapped twice again. "Hello? Please don't make me take your phone away."

"Sorry, Ms. B," said Stephanie.

"She's afraid her boyfriend is looking at other girls."

Stephanie elbowed Natasha in the ribs. "He's not my boyfriend."

"Whatever he is," British said, taking a deep breath to tamp down her amusement, "he can wait until we finish going over the rules I just received for the STEM-Off." She was met with a round of groans as she extracted the folded piece of paper she had printed off from the superintendent this morning. "You guys are familiar with competitions. There are five groups. You, the boys from Southwood Middle, two high school teams and one group from the elementary school."

An almost collective *aww* and *how cute* filled the room.

British looked up and cleared her throat. She held her hand out in front of Kathleen to turn over the handheld game system and continued without missing a beat in reading the directions. From what she gathered, the competition would be set up like one of the baking challenges she'd watched on the Food Network. There would be two challenges: a small round and a bigger round incorporating each faction of STEM. If they won the small STEM challenge, they could add another member to their team for the bigger STEM challenge. British liked the girls to do work on simple everyday items people didn't realize used science, technology, engineering or math. The girls needed to brainstorm their ideas. Once they got into that room, the teachers were no longer able to help. Teachers would be designated seats behind the judges. At Districts, there'd be no teachers at all. The teams were going to have to come up with a variety of supplies needed for the Southwood competition and be prepared for any task they were given.

"Can we come up with a new video game, one where the girl is the heroine? That way we can cover engineering and tech, and she can be a scientist," Kathleen spoke up. "Ya know?"

"Considering a lot of judges on the Christmas Advisory Council are women—" British said, trying to focus on the page in front of her. The tiny hairs on the back of her neck rose. Odd that she sensed him there. The only presence she'd felt before was Christian's. It also helped to see that Donovan managed to evoke that familiar, googly-eyed gaze not just from women at the Cupcakery but also from impressionable teenage girls. "Mr. Ravens?" British called out. "We're trying to brainstorm down here."

Not caring, Donovan stepped through the half-closed French doors, oblivious as to how his tight white shirt hugged his muscular frame or the way the well-worn denim hugged those thick thighs and tapered waist. He claimed to work in the office at Ravens Cosmetics but if she didn't know any better British would swear the man simply worked out for a living.

"I don't mean to pry." His deep voice chilled her bones.

"Of course not," British mumbled, rubbing her left hand over her right forearm to keep the goose bumps away.

"I didn't realize you all were going to be meeting here in the library," Donovan went on to say.

"Did you need a book, Mr. Ravens?" Stephanie asked, getting up from her spot. "Or maybe a magazine?"

British shook her head at the way the girls fawned over him. "I told you already, Mr. Ravens—"

"Donovan," he corrected and gave the girls a wink. "'Mr. Ravens' sounds so stuffy, like my brothers."

The girls giggled and British sighed. "Okay, if you say so, but I warned you we'd be here working."

"I understand—" Donovan nodded "—and I would be remiss if I didn't intervene here."

Hands on her hips, British cocked a brow up at him. Was he always this tall? "How would you like to butt in?"

Another round of giggles.

"I heard you mention something called a Christmas Advisory Council."

Something in Donovan's tone irked her. He probably didn't believe such a thing existed. "We're a small town, sure, but we take the upcoming holiday season seriously around here."

"I don't doubt you." Like he had earlier, Donovan held his arms out in surrender in front of her. At least, she thought it was surrender. The bulging muscles of his biceps swelling against the cotton fabric of his shirt distracted her. British's mouth went dry for a moment. "What?" Her voice cracked.

"I didn't say anything," he said with a grin. Damn it. He knew she was ogling him. "But if you all are competing at an event where the judges are gung ho on the holidays, maybe it would benefit you guys to come up with some ideas for the season."

"OMG!" Kathleen shrieked. "I have been dying to code to a Christmas song. I've got all the equipment and lights already. When the song comes on, we can make the white lights match the singer, green lights for the chorus, and red lights if there's like a drum solo. It will be so cool."

"You need to do it to my favorite song," said Natasha, turning to British and Donovan. "It's old. Maybe you've heard of it? Mariah Carey's 'All I Want for Christmas.'"

"I believe I have," said Donovan. "How about you, Ms. B?"

"Once or twice." British clapped her hands together. "All right, let's thank Mr. Donovan and let him get on his way."

"Oh, don't worry about it." Donovan leaned against the door frame. "I wasn't doing anything."

"Really, the girls don't need the distraction," British said through gritted teeth.

"Aw, Ms. B," the girls whined. "Please, can he stay?"

One could only imagine their parents; their homes must be filled with puppies. How was she supposed to say no to them? "Fine," she groaned, "but just stay out of the way. You know what they say about cooks?"

"Not cooks," replied Donovan, "but I do know what Chef Jessilyn has to say about you."

British elbowed Donovan in his six-pack stomach, knowing good and well it didn't hurt. "Be quiet."

"Miss Jessilyn makes the best cookies," Natasha added into the conversation. "I wonder if she has any."

Donovan scratched the back of his head. "I saw her pulling out a batch when I put up my lunch dishes."

And that was all it took for the STEM for GRITS team to take off out of the room, hurling their promises to be right back behind them.

They took off with such a rush Donovan spun around after being hit by one and pushed out of the room by another. Then with the last two he was spun back into the room and pushed against British.

Now alone with Donovan, British took a step away from him. "Thanks for that," she snarled. "Do you realize how hard it was to get them all on the same page?"

Mouth opened in stunned disbelief, Donovan shook his head. "Those girls need to be on the track team."

"A few are," British replied. She sighed and took a seat on the couch. Donovan followed her and sat on the arm of an overstuffed chair.

"Donovan, this may be hard for you to understand, but the girls are in a time crunch and they need to focus."

"What did I do to distract them?"

British waved her hand at his attire. "Seriously?"

Donovan crossed his arms over his chest in feigned modesty. "I feel so cheap."

All of a sudden British laughed. "I'm sorry if I am testy."

"Just a little bit," Donovan said, lifting his large hand and measuring an inch with his thumb and forefinger. For a man who worked behind a desk at a powerful company, Donovan somehow bore several scars on his hand. When he realized she was staring, he dropped his hand to his side. "It's cool," he said with a nod. "I get what you're trying to do and I admire it. Such leadership."

If only he'd left off the last part. The compliment triggered an alert in her. "Do not offer me a job at Ravens Cosmetics."

"May I at least ask why?"

"I'm a teacher, Donovan. Clearly, by me being here with the girls, you can see I am highly dedicated to them."

"All right, fine," he said.

Somehow she knew the discussion wasn't over.

"What happens when you win this competition?" Donovan asked.

"Well, bragging rights…" British began but got distracted for a moment when Donovan cast a smile as if he understood. She felt her cheeks heat. "The current director is a bit of a sexist jerk when it comes to women in science," she explained.

Donovan wiggled his brows. "Want me to rough him up a bit?"

"Thanks, but no thanks. We're molding the minds of impressionable young ladies," she said. "So by winning, we would get the respect of the science department at Southwood Middle School and hopefully we'll be able to move our practice space to the school, especially since our rec center burned down."

"You're not in the school?"

British shook her head. "I usually meet with the girls at the old Southwood rec center after school. They come over and we work on projects. The only reason we're here is that the storm last week blew a transformer and the sparks set off a fire in the building and a few of the homes. Two of the team members and their families are staying here, courtesy of Ramon and Kenzie."

"I remember them from last year—" he nodded "—at the beauty pageant held here."

"Yes, Miss Southwood." British nodded, as well.

"I won't even ask if you know about pageants, since you seem to hate makeup," said Donovan with a laugh. He rose from his seat on the armchair.

British's eyes roamed the seat of his pants. What was wrong with her? Her students were right in the other room, squealing over cookies while she sat in here mentally undressing this man.

"Why don't you have your science group at the school?" Donovan clasped his hands behind his back and strolled over to the bay window.

Glad he couldn't see her face, British frowned, hating to recall Cam and the monopolizing of the science department. "Let's just say there's already a group in there."

"Schools usually pay for materials, right?" Donovan asked, half turning to face her.

Here comes the question that always throws people. British nodded.

"Does the school pay for your rec center activities?"

British shook her head and shrugged. "No. And yes, I am the one buying all the supplies."

"On a teacher's salary?" Donovan fully turned to face her. "It's been a while since I went to school, but the last I checked, teachers didn't work for the glorious salary."

"My husband left me some money," British explained. "Every dime I received has gone into the facility and the girls."

"You have faith, don't you?"

"Sometimes that's all you have."

Silence fell between them. Donovan stared at British. Finally, British rolled her eyes. "Well, I'd better go gather the girls up so they can get to work."

Donovan crossed the room and reached British before she stepped out the French doors. "If there's anything I can do, or anything you need, I want you to know you can come to me."

"That's mighty generous of you, Donovan," said British. "But why?"

"Let's just say my faith just may have been restored."

Thankfully the girls were able to focus over the following twenty-four hours. On a few occasions Donovan found a reason to make himself seen whether it was to come into the library, where they plotted their ideas, or to run through the trail in the back—shirtless—when they practiced experiments. British couldn't put the blame all on the girls for being easily distracted. She, too, lost track of time when she realized she could see through the window of the hotel gym and catch Donovan working out.

Knowing the STEM-Off was coming up, though, British was able to finally focus. To practice as many possible tasks the committee may give them, she shouted out different ideas for experiments in science, technology, engineering and math, and timed them. The girls brainstormed on what to build, including the list of things they'd need. They wanted to impress the judges, but also to truly learn something in the process.

For a few of the challenges some wanted to assemble a small-scale trampoline and show the parents of the Christmas Advisory Council how it was made. Natasha wanted to aim for a homemade vending machine. And Kathleen said she could build a coding game without using a computer. The afternoon had been so productive, British didn't see the need for more brainstorming later. That worked out perfectly for the girls, who were eager to head out to enjoy the last days of the fall festival.

Since hell hadn't frozen over, British continued to have her meals away from Magnolia Palace. No way she'd allow Jessilyn to cook for her. Even now, the eye daggers flew as British came down the stairs and crossed paths with the chef. Brushing off the icy stare, British twisted her hair into a bun and secured it at the top of her head. Before she made it to the front desk, she heard a high-pitched squeal of laughter from one of her girls, which echoed through the halls of the upscale boutique hotel. British headed toward the library to get the girls to settle down. She was surprised at what she found looking through the glass doors.

For a guy who'd wanted to be left alone for the week, Donovan Ravens had a funny way of showing it. British cocked her head to the side and folded her arms across the front of the lightweight sweater she'd worn in preparation for this evening's temperature drop.

"So you think Quandriguez is a jerk to me because he likes me?" Stephanie asked Donovan.

Donovan leaned against the door frame of the sun-room with his back to the lake and took a deep breath. "I don't really know the fellow to make that statement, so all I can tell you right now is that a lot of boys—and hear me out when I say 'boys'—don't know how to use their words to express how they feel."

"Maybe he's not being mean, or I'm reading it wrong. His older brother is deaf and his baby sister, too. Maybe he's stressed."

A dry chuckle escaped Donovan's throat. "*Never* make an excuse for a boy or a man. Stress is never a reason to be mean."

"Did you ever ignore a girl because you liked her?"

Interested in the answer, British perked up. Donovan struck her as the type of man who didn't have to say a word to get a woman to notice him. He just needed to stare at her one good time with those piercing light brown eyes, maybe even lick his lips together, and a woman would go crazy or at least feel a trail of goose bumps traveling down her arm. British shivered and smoothed her hand over her biceps.

"You just keep doing what you've been doing," Donovan went on to say.

"Even if it means I should not do my best at this competition?"

Wait, what? No way in the world would she ever tell one of her girls to dumb herself down for a boy. From where she stood, British could see Donovan's jaw twitch. He rolled his head from side to side, causing a crack in his neck.

"Look here," he said to Stephanie. "There is nothing se—" Donovan stopped while British cringed. Maybe it was time she stepped in to end this conversation. But Donovan recovered and continued. "There is nothing more attractive than a woman with a brain."

"Are your girlfriends smart?"

"I don't do girlfriends," Donovan quipped, "but if I did, I'd like her to have a brain and not be worried about hurting my feelings."

"Ms. B doesn't mind hurting your feelings," Stephanie offered. British narrowed her eyes. "And she is smart."

"And beautiful," Donovan mused.

British's heart thumped against her ribs. This was so silly, to feel giddy knowing he found her attractive.

"But we're talking about you and—"

"Quandriguez," said the precocious teen.

"Well, if this Quandriguez can't see how wonderful and smart you are right now, he isn't worth your time."

"Really?" Stephanie squealed in delight.

"Scout's honor," said Donovan as he straightened.

British couldn't see what he was doing but Stephanie giggled. "That's not the Scout symbol."

"It isn't?"

"There's not a boy in Southwood who hasn't been through the Scouts," said Stephanie. "I know that salute."

Donovan's chuckle at being caught made British snicker and expose her location.

"Miss British?" Donovan called her name and the deep sound of his voice sent a chill down her spine. "Is that you?"

"I'm sorry," said British as she stepped around the corner. "It wasn't my intent to eavesdrop on y'all's conversation."

Stephanie came to her feet from her spot in the plush, white-cushioned chair by the bay window. "It's cool," she said. "Mr. Donovan was just giving me some good advice."

"Followed by the wrong salute?" British crossed her arms over her chest. The thin green sweater suddenly felt too warm and itchy.

Donovan had dressed appropriately for the fall weather. The long-sleeved, garnet T-shirt hugged a well-toned body. "We were just discussing the age-old debate about if a boy is mean to you it must mean he likes you."

Considering the fact that Donovan was always a source of joy to be around, British realized where she stood with him.

With a bow, Donovan pressed his hand over his heart. "*I*, for one, am against that theory."

"Are you?"

"It sets girls up to accept abuse or mistreatment early on," Stephanie explained.

Such a professional tone from the girl who chewed gum to a rhythmic beat in class caused British to quirk a brow and shift her stare between the two of them. "Interesting."

"It is," replied Donovan. "I'm a firm believer in being sweeter."

"Well," Stephanie giggled, "I'm going to find my friends. But Mr. D—" she pointed her fingers into a gun shape "—don't forget about my idea."

"I'll pay for your patent once you work out the details."

Stephanie squealed and took off with such a force that the door swung shut, leaving the two adults alone.

British shook her head and looked at Donovan. "Dare I ask?"

"That," he said, pointing toward the exit through which Stephanie disappeared, "is Ravens Cosmetics' future secret weapon."

"What did she pitch?"

"An app for phones that will show a model and, if I've got this right, transposes the makeup on the model's made-up face so the girls can follow a trace or something."

"The Trace-A-Face?" British asked with a snicker.

"That might have been the name."

British shook her head. "I am so glad she's here this week. This way she can believe in herself without makeup."

"Hey, now," Donovan said, clutching his heart, "makeup is my livelihood."

"You mean selling foundation to cover women's flaws?" Back when she did pageants, British met tons of girls with such low self-esteem once the makeup came off. They didn't understand pimples were a part of growing up, not the end of the world.

Donovan shook his head. "If you think we had a product like that, don't you think I'd use it on this?" With that, Donovan aimed his index finger at the X-shaped scar across his face. The dark beard across his chiseled jawline covered part of the mark but she knew it was there. Her fingers twitched and her heart lurched.

"I—I wasn't trying to…"

"Don't act like you haven't noticed it, British," he replied coolly and winked. "It's okay. Everyone stares at it. I catch them often."

British shrugged her shoulders. "People aren't taught not to stare these days."

"Curiosity is human nature." He gave a quick shrug of his shoulders.

"But still."

"Don't you want to know how I got it?"

"I assumed it was a car accident." British strolled

over to the floor-to-ceiling bookshelf. She switched a few of the modern classics around, including the collection of Brontë sisters. She cast a glance over her shoulder.

Dark, thick brows rose with surprise. "Really? Most people believe I received it due to a lover's quarrel."

For some reason Donovan closed the gap between them before she even realized their proximity and reached down to smooth a stray hair back behind her ear. British turned her face into the palm of his hand. Her eyes closed as she forgot where she was for a moment. Another place. Another time…she might have let him kiss her because that came next when a man stood this close. Her heart slammed against her rib cage, reminding her of the needs she possessed as a woman. Her body ached for his touch. Embarrassed by her desire, British took a step back and cleared her throat.

"Well, I don't know you well enough to say if you're scoundrel enough for such an act of revenge."

"A scoundrel?" Donovan pulled *Wuthering Heights* off a smaller bookshelf's row of the *Sugar Plum Ballerinas* series and placed it beside the set British had just rearranged. Him knowing the difference between the books earned him an ounce of respect from British. "But you would say a car crash?"

"My husband received a similar scar when his face hit the steering wheel at a right angle."

Donovan stepped backward. "I'm sorry."

"Don't be," she whispered. The knot threatening her throat eased quicker than normal. "Enough of this sad talk. I didn't mean to eavesdrop, but I was on my way out for dinner and—"

"Wait, you're not eating here?" Donovan cut her off

and sniffed the air. "Chef Jessilyn is making homemade chili since the temperature is dropping."

"Not on my life." British laughed.

"There's a history between you two," Donovan observed, pointing his finger at her.

"Let's just say not all students hold me in such high regard as the GRITS team does."

That got a deep laugh out of Donovan. "Hard to believe it, but I'll let you tell the story over dinner, if you'll share it with me."

Cocking her head to the side, British stroked her chin. "Have you had a tour of Southwood?"

"I've been meaning to, especially now," he said.

British narrowed her eyes at him. "I'm afraid to ask."

"Had you showed up for the wonderful lunch Chef prepared for us," he teased with a wink, "you would have heard the girls talking about the snatched—"

"Snatched?" Tears began to form in the corners of her eyes at Donovan's accurate lingo. This man ran a billion-dollar company and spoke fluent Teen.

"Yes," Donovan boasted with a pat on his broad chest. "I'm cool. I know the haps."

"Okay, Mr. Cool." British dabbed the corner of her right eye with her finger.

"Anyway, the girls were telling me about original gifts I can get my nieces here, other than shipping them cupcakes, which I am still contemplating since I'm *stanning* them."

"Dear Lord," she giggled, "please stop."

"What? You don't like my Eminem reference?" Proud of himself, Donovan nodded his chin at her for emphasis of his coolness.

As a teacher, she'd heard all the latest slang. "Stanning," derived from an Eminem song, now referred to someone obsessed with something. At last year's *fleek*, as in being on point, British had stopped trying to keep up with today's youth.

"Did you learn these terms from your young girl-friends?"

Licking his lips, Donovan cocked his head to the side. "We've established our age differences and you might be the youngest woman I've seriously been interested in."

Breath caught in her throat for a moment, then she remembered that he wanted her to work for his company as a spokesmodel. For years British wanted to be more than a pretty face. How would it look if she were to suddenly become the face of a popular cosmetics line? Donovan barked up the wrong tree with this proposal. British responded with an eye-roll and changed the subject. "I pegged you as an internet shopper."

"I can be," he answered, moving to sit on the arm of the couch, "but as CFO of a major company, I don't mind shopping around for a deal, especially if it's a one of a kind."

"Wouldn't it be easier if you got all the ladies the same gift, that way you don't have to keep track of them?"

"One of these days I'm going to surprise you," Donovan declared.

British studied his face and ignored the way he made her heart beat—all erratic like a schoolgirl's. He rose to his feet and stretched. A sliver of washboard ab peeked when his shirt rose and British unapologetically stared. What? The man was good-looking, she argued with herself. Her friends—hell, even her in-laws—were ready for her to move on. And British knew she too missed the comfort of a man.

"So what's going on outside of Magnolia Palace? Anything good?"

The realization that this playboy was the perfect man for her to get her groove on hit her. No family in town. Only here for a while. Everything about his body said he was a fantastic lover. Near fainting, British grabbed hold of the wall. "Dear Lord, you're in for a treat. I happen to know the best view in town. Want to come with me?"

Donovan raised his left brow and pondered her question.

Embarrassed, British closed her eyes and shook her head, admitting to herself that his blatant flirting had intrigued her. Maybe it was time to start delving into her desires for another man. Now nervous for admitting she wanted him, British wrung her hands together. The rock Christian had placed on her finger scraped against her hand. Vonna was right. He would not want her living like a nun. He might not be gung ho on her choice in a playboy like Donovan, but he was a start… and, more important, he was temporary. "I'll be right back," she told him.

When she went upstairs to her room, British hoped she'd played it cool. Something about the way he'd flirted with her made her…dance…the same way she did when she bit into something delicious. Giggling, British took a long look at herself in the mirror and shook her head, wondering what Christian would think of her now.

She twisted off her ring to set it on a lace doily. Donovan was the complete opposite of Christian. Christian had wanted nothing more than to be in a monogamous relationship for as long a time as he was permitted on earth. Donovan, however, was the type of person to get with as many women as possible while he lived on earth. Maybe that's what she needed. A no-strings fling. Perfect. Going out to the festival with Donovan was sure to cause people to gossip. So what? The grandfather clock downstairs chimed six. Satisfied with herself, British headed to the door, then turned back around to snatch her ring off the dresser. *Baby steps, British. Baby steps.*

"You promise you're not leading me to this roadkill diner you mentioned the other day?" Donovan asked British, within less than a half hour of leaving Magnolia Palace.

Even with his eyes focused on the long, dark road ahead of them, Donovan felt the burning sensation of the side-eye daggers British shot him from the passenger seat. Under one of the lone streetlights, he turned and winked.

"I can't guarantee there won't be any vittles like that," she began, clucking her tongue against the roof of her mouth. "I will say if the sign above the counter says 'mystery meat' and it's deep-fried…don't eat it."

Donovan's laugh rattled the interior of the Jaguar. "I'll make note of it."

Bright lights filled the town square. The only thing on Donovan's mind the other day had been getting another batch of cupcakes. He hadn't bothered looking around town; otherwise he might have noticed the carnival equipment. A man carrying a small child over his shoulders waved at Donovan's car and pointed to a space, where a convertible's taillights flickered. Donovan let his window down to wave acknowledgment and thanks at the same time.

The smells of popcorn, smoked meats and cotton candy permeated the inside of the car. Donovan's stomach growled. "I guess a man can't live on fresh chocolate-chip cupcakes alone," he joked.

"Well, let's hurry up and find you something recognizable to eat."

As he flipped the turn signal for the parking space, British gazed out the passenger-side window. Was she looking for someone? Since she still wore her wedding ring, he doubted she was checking for a boyfriend. Once the space became free, Donovan pulled forward and backed into it, another car allowing Donovan to park before driving by. Maybe it was his imagination, but British seemed to use the opportune time to duck her head to unclick her seat belt. That same old suspicious radar dinged in the back of his head. She was hiding something from him.

"Hey, Ms. B," someone shouted in the parking lot.

British squinted her eyes and tried to recognize the voice. "Hey, Mario."

Donovan recognized Mario and Dario Crowne. Their older brother, Dominic, was a good friend of the family's. Dominic's brothers and sister, Alisha, were always in town from South Florida over at the house in the Overtown neighborhood for epic parties. "Hi, boys."

"Who's that you've got with you? Oh snap," Dario said, shielding his eyes from the blaze of the setting sun. "Donovan?"

"Hey, twins," Donovan called out with a head nod. "I thought I heard you were in Southwood now."

Dario and Mario came over and greeted Donovan with a hug and handshake. They talked for a few minutes before a few young ladies walked by and caught their attention.

"I am about to walk into my hometown festival with

a celebrity, aren't I?" British teased, elbowing Donovan in the ribs.

Giving a shallow cough, Donovan casually draped his arm over her shoulder. A part of him wondered if this would show he was staking a claim on her. He had no right but being this close to her felt natural. So caught up in his thoughts, Donovan heard the honk of a car horn in enough time to pull British up onto the curb. The movement had been so quick but they lingered in each other's embrace for ten heartbeats or more. They broke apart when a whirl of wind from a ride blew over their head followed by the screams of women, children and men.

British stepped out of his embrace with a shiver. "Where do you want to start? Rides? Or did you say you were scared?"

Donovan cleared his throat and puffed out his chest. "I never said either. But I'm not a big fan of roller coasters."

"You don't seriously think something bad can happen, now do you?"

"You mean get stuck upside down and fall out?" Donovan waved off the notion with a healthy dose of sarcasm and a *pshaw*. "Sure, all those news stories were wrong."

"They were wrong for not telling the full story." British rolled her eyes. "Majority of the injuries happen because of people not following the rules."

"Let me guess, there's a science behind roller coasters?" Donovan joked.

"Engineering." British beamed. "You've been paying attention to my lessons with the girls."

"Maybe a little."

"Well, then you'll realize the reporters are sensationalizing the stories. Have you ever noticed they come out right before the brink of the summer season? I swear it's just to scare people."

"Scare?" Donovan held his left hand out with his palm upward. "Warn? Caution?" he said, ticking off more synonyms of the word on each left finger with his long, right index finger. "I don't see the difference."

"You don't?" British gaped.

"And you know what else I don't see?"

"What?"

The familiar whirl whizzed over their heads. Donovan looked up in time to see what looked like a spinning fireball zoom through the air inches above his head. The gush of wind from the roller coaster was so forceful it whipped British's hair all around her face. The ride went around and around in circles. Patrons screamed with thrills. A cell phone and a hat landed in the gated area around the base of the ride.

"You won't see me getting on that thing." Donovan folded his arms across his chest.

"Chicken," British teased and tugged his arm loose to grab his hand. "C'mon, let's go get on the ride."

Donovan stood still. "Wait…how about if we get a bite to eat from the mystery meat stand?"

British followed his gaze to the caravan of food trucks parked alongside the town square. Serpentine lines wrapped each vehicle. The one with the shortest line came from the truck with the sign You'll Never Guess. Despite what she'd warned him about in the car, the smells were delicious and tempting. Donovan took a step in the direction but British squeezed his hand.

"I can't do that to you. Let's go find something else to eat."

"See, and here I was all game." Donovan's shoulders relaxed and he felt the blood pump and course through his veins when she winked at him.

"And then we'll get on the rides," British said with a laugh before pulling him around the festival. "Unless you're afraid you're going to scream and cry."

"I don't cry," he said flatly.

Since this was the last night of the festival, everything was half off. British didn't argue with Donovan when he stepped in front of her to pay for the tickets or for the cotton candy and corn dogs they ate while they walked around.

Her students stopped her every now and then, and British moved off to the side to have a conference with some of the parents who hadn't been able to make it to school so far this year. He didn't mind. Donovan had dated some models who were also single mothers, and he'd heard how hard it was for a working mom to meet with her kid's teachers. Of course, they'd mention this in the hope Donovan would be able to get them a full-time gig working at Ravens Cosmetics or to settle down with him and live the life of luxury.

"I think I am the one walking around with the celebrity," Donovan taunted when British finished with a parent and student. The on-the-spot conference had ended with the mother profusely thanking and thanking British for her patience, and British and the young man high-fiving each other.

Under the pink glow of a ride, British blushed. "Well, I did grow up here." As she waved her hand like a showcase hostess, her eyes widened and Donovan swore she cursed under her breath.

"And I'm surprised we haven't—" His words were cut off.

"Quick." British grabbed hold of Donovan's hand and tugged him hard toward their first roller coaster of the evening. "Let's get on a ride."

A pulse of fear jolted through him. The last thing he wanted to do was to give up his masculinity card for screaming like a child and fainting, like he'd seen on a YouTube video his sister Dana's kids, his nieces and nephews, showed him. "Wait, what?"

Fortunately for him, every death-defying ride British dragged him to had lines. The folks of the town had come out in droves. Donovan sighed in relief at the Ferris wheel. The ticket-taker ripped their tickets in two and lifted the plastic rope for them to enter.

The available cart was a two-seater and Donovan did not mind. Without giving it much thought, he stretched his arm around British and heat rose from her shoulders to the crook of his elbow. Donovan rested his long legs against the foot rail. The compartment rocked forward. British sat on the inside, using his body as a shield from someone in the crowd.

"Are we sure this is safe?" He turned his light brown eyes toward her.

"You're afraid?"

"Nah," Donovan chuckled and sat back in his seat. "I rank placing myself in unnecessary danger right up there with jumping out of a perfectly functioning airplane."

"You can skydive over in Peachville," British offered. "I mean, if you want."

"I don't," he replied quickly. The sounds below grew quieter. The occasional roar of the fireball roller coaster and screams from the other rides rang out.

"So who were you hiding from?"

Chapter 5

British had hoped Donovan hadn't noticed her paranoia. Spotting Cam in the parking lot had set off a chain reaction. Cam, she could handle, basically because he'd been leaving as they'd pulled into the lot. No, the biggest fear for British had been her family, whose calls she still hadn't bothered returning since she arrived at Magnolia Palace. With the Thanksgiving holiday rapidly approaching, her mother hounded her for confirmation that she would be coming over to the house.

As the baby of the Woodburys, British had grown up with a mother and four other brothers and sisters who thought they were her parents. It was only a matter of time before they all ran into each other at the festival. British spotted her six-foot-tall mom by the basketball game shooting hoops and racking up on the prizes with three giant teddy bears already, probably one for each granddaughter. At least, up high in the air, British was out of earshot and eyesight of Joan Woodbury…just not Donovan's questioning stare.

"If you must know who I am trying to avoid," British said, licking her lips and tasting the sweet leftover sugar from her cotton candy, "I am hiding from my mother."

Donovan closed his eyes and nodded. "Completely understandable."

British glanced up to see a smirk competing with the grin across his face. When she did, she elbowed him.

"What?" Donovan asked mockingly. "I always get on death traps to avoid my mom."

"I'm not avoiding-avoiding her," British replied. "I am just…well, um, not ready to bump into her."

"Because you're with me?" Donovan asked, his hand covering his jawline while his fingers absently brushed against his visible scar.

The vulnerable stroke touched British and she felt sorry for him. Didn't he realize how sexy it made him? The question astonished her and her heart lurched in her chest.

British twisted her wedding ring around on her finger. Just because she was widowed, that did not make her blind. The words of her mother-in-law rang in her head, which British shook. British wanted Donovan but not in a long-term way. If he wanted more, well, then Donovan was not the man for her. But she didn't want him to think it was because of his scar. She'd just traveled down the marital road before and once was enough.

"Not necessarily," British said. "With Thanksgiving coming up, I haven't been in the mood for being around family."

"Oh yeah, I keep forgetting," said Donovan. "I need to make a note to myself to have Ramon send the skeleton staff working home on my dime."

"You're in the generous mood," British said.

"Maybe the holidays put me in one," he answered. "Why does it have you in a sour one?"

"Christian loved everything about the Thanksgiving week." British sighed.

The Ferris wheel moved a notch. Donovan wrapped his hand around her shoulder. "This time of year must be difficult and you probably want to be left alone."

"Not alone, just not smothered. Christian's been gone for five years and every holiday my mom and siblings treat me like I am a child, so I ditch them whenever I can. Does that sound weird?"

"No." Donovan shook his head. "Trust me, I needed to get out of South Florida without letting my family know what was going on in my life."

"Bad breakup?" British guessed. He confirmed his answer with a quick nod. She imagined some poor girl clinging to his pant leg as he tried to leave a room.

"Not only bad," said Donovan, "but caught on camera."

British's hands flew to her mouth to cover her half laugh and half gasp. "What?"

"My sister insisted on having the family become more public so our brand could gain traction on social media," Donovan began. "This somehow was turned into a reality television segment on all of us. My portion happened to catch my current…" He gulped down whatever word followed and even turned a sickly olive color.

"Girlfriend?" British supplied and wiggled her brows. "Is it so hard to say the word?"

"'Girlfriend' sounds so committed." Donovan shivered. "We only knew each other for a little over a month."

"A month?" British's mouth gaped. "Don't you believe in love at first sight?"

"That would imply I believe in love."

Disappointment rose in British's chest. There'd be no love between them. But then again, that might just be what she needed. "A month is plenty of time to fall in love, though."

"No, I think I'm going to give women two before I even consider it."

Even though British felt the idea of a romp in the hay with Donovan was what she might need to satisfy this uncontrollable urge she felt when she was with him, that disappointment bubble lingered in her chest.

"But, truthfully, I almost brought her with me this weekend until…" Donovan started to continue but stopped himself.

I'm glad he didn't.

"I'm glad I didn't," Donovan said, seemingly reading her thoughts. "I wasn't too sure about things with her. I thought maybe if we came here together I'd know where things were heading. I'd even made plans for her parents to meet us for Thanksgiving dinner. I guess that says a lot about me." Donovan chuckled at himself and looked down at British. She gave him a frown. "I'm sorry. I just dodged a bullet by having to hang out with them. My family is crazy enough. I don't need to add to it."

The Ravens family drama was public knowledge. There'd been an attempted family corporate takeover or something and a long-lost daughter coming back into their lives to save the day.

"Two months or not, I don't think she would have made the cut to be my…" His words trailed off and the hue of his skin turned greener than when she'd teased him about going on the upside-down roller coaster.

British nudged her elbow against his solid rib cage. "Aren't you too old to think girls have cooties?"

"Not cooties, but ulterior motives."

The fact he didn't finish what the current girlfriend had or hadn't done did not go unnoticed. So what was the relationship now? He was here in Southwood, alone, and she was elsewhere. British rolled her eyes, mad at herself for the surge of jealousy. "I guess I fell into that category."

"As in a girl*friend*?" he sang with a grin.

"Oh, be serious." British leaned her weight forward and tilted their cart.

"All right, now." Donovan unwrapped his arm from around her shoulders and grabbed hold of the bar with his large hands until his knuckles turned white. "Stop before you make us fall."

British stopped and laughed. "I'm sorry. That was horrible of me." She turned in the seat, pulling the inside of her sole into her left knee to better face Donovan. "I'll stop."

"You're a rotten girl*friend*." Donovan drawled the word with a teasing smile and let go of the bar to face her. She gave him a death stare matched with narrowed eyes and pinched lips. "Oh, so you're *not* a girl that's a friend?"

"You sound like my students," British chided.

"Given the fact you just commented on my age, I'll take that as a compliment."

Just then they reached the top of the Ferris wheel. It gave British the opportunity to show Donovan the sights of the town starting with the Four Points Park, which united their neighboring towns—Peachville, Black Wolf Creek and Samaritan—over their treetops. Though British had no idea how long Donovan planned to be in Southwood, she promised him that summertime not only offered the sweetest smells with the peach orchards but also a fabulous light show from the firefly forest. And until now she hadn't realized Donovan's arm rested around the back of her seat, resting on her shoulders— or that she'd nestled herself against him.

"And out yonder, right next to the middle school, is the high school," British said, pointing in the distance.

Donovan cleared his throat. "Is that where you and Christian met?"

Not sure how to answer, British glanced upward. "I've never been on a date where a man wanted to hear about my husband."

Grinning under the stars, Donovan looked down and winked. "So we're on a date."

"Oh… I…" She was stumped to find the words. Maybe if she lifted the lap bar she could escape this awkward moment. They weren't that far off the ground.

"Relax." Donovan squeezed her shoulder. "I'm just giving you a hard time. I get what you're saying—you wouldn't date a guy like me."

"Shut up," British laughed.

"Relax," said Donovan again. He pulled her close. "You're from a small town. I get it. You're widowed and I'm guessing being seen with me is going to get people to talk."

"Again, not just people, my family. My nosy family," she added.

"I think somewhere in there you did not deny being attracted to me," he teased.

British gulped and shuddered at the same time. "I'd have to be blind to not see you're attractive. I just…"

"Seriously," he went on, "I am not trying to get married or anything. Not now, not ever."

A sharp pain pierced her heart. "Don't knock it until you try it."

Now it was Donovan's turn to shudder. "I'll pass. I am too old and I'm set in my ways. I've heard my sisters complain about their in-laws and having to feel obligated to spend time with them over the holidays. If I don't want to be around someone, I just don't deal with them anymore."

"What a shame. Being a perpetual bachelor seems so lonely," British said, her lips turning into a frown. Her heart ached listening to him. "I loved being married. There's something comforting about coming home at the end of the day to someone waiting for you, eager to hear about your day, even if you know your time together might be limited."

There was no questioning his curious look so British shared a story about Christian, about how they'd met and his heart problems—including about their time being ironically living life carefully, only to be cut short due to a deer in the middle of the road. British couldn't believe how easy it was for her to open up about Christian. And she appreciated him not coddling her or feeling sorry for her, either. In turn, Donovan shared what it was like to grow up in a famous family and never knowing if he could trust the women who claimed they saw past the scar were interested in him, or secretly out for a modeling job or his fortune. It didn't make her feel good about coming to Magnolia Palace to butter him up. The poor man never came across a woman who didn't want something from him.

"This town is nice," Donovan commented when the conversation lulled.

"Is that sarcasm I hear?" British asked, looking up at him.

"Of course not," he said with a lazy smile and a

wave of his free hand. "I live in Miami. It's the town that never sleeps."

British cleared her throat. "I'm pretty sure that's New York City."

"You're the teacher," he said, shrugging. "But back to Southwood. I like it. It's growing on me."

"I'm waiting for you to say it's quaint."

"*Quaint* isn't a bad thing, Ms. B." He paused and chuckled to make sure his formality pushed her buttons. For his benefit, British huffed. "My sister-in-law grew up here," said Donovan. "Are you familiar with the Mas Beauty School?"

Everyone in the Four Points area knew about the famous Mas building, once run by Sadie Baldwin. Decades ago, Mas was a cosmetology school for young girls who came and lived in part of the old brick house in dorm-like rooms and used other portions of the home for school work. They learned how to do makeup and hair and even create makeup, all to land them sustainable jobs for their futures. Back when British's goals were to become Miss America or Miss USA, she wanted to learn all the ins and outs of the business; there hadn't been a summer British didn't spend studying cosmetology. British prided herself on being a makeup expert. She'd perfected the wingtip, mastered the glue for her lashes so well that she could place them on her own lids without a mirror and with just one hand. But she also wanted to know what went into the glue and its effects on a person's skin. Spending time at Mas helped redirect British's focus in science. Of course, it had been scientists who made British feel self-conscious about her makeup.

"I remember Zoe," British finally answered. She smiled fondly and decided not to share how fascinated

Zoe had been with the success of the Ravens family. Donovan's face filled with pride talking about his great-grandparents and how they'd come up with the first Ravens products and created what became a conglomerate in today's world.

"You know my brother married her after meeting her at Magnolia Palace," he said, filling the silence.

"Yep." British's throat went dry. "There is something romantic about the hotel."

The higher their car went, the smaller the people below became and the more intimate the space between them became. British glanced up at Donovan at the same time he looked at her. The moment was spontaneous, especially for her. With half-closed eyes, she arched her neck and Donovan leaned down. The air thinned. Her breath caught in her throat and her heart pounded against her ribs.

From below a heavy thud of the high-striker carnival game thundered up through the sky as a silver ball traveled along a metal post at their eye level as their car began to lower. The bell rang out, echoing between them. British pulled away and cleared her throat. Their ride slowed to a disappointing stop. Had she wanted more time with Donovan? No, not at all, she thought as she glanced from side to side to find her extra-tall mother. No sign. More than likely Joan had headed over to the grocery store to buy every sweet potato left in town in order to make enough pies to feed everyone.

Donovan turned his head. British studied his profile. His jaw twitched under his close-cropped beard. His long nose jutted out with a slight bend as if it had been broken at one point. A part of her wondered if it happened in the accident that had left him with the scar or if it had come from a brawl. Donovan seemed to relish his playboy status. Perhaps he'd pissed off a few people along the way.

"I guess I need to thank you for not killing me on the ride," Donovan joked, stepping off the car once the ride-handler lifted the lap bar. He turned and extended his hand for British to take. She obliged but not before glancing around the park. A teensy spark set off at their touch. Logic told her it was the combination of the cold air and them sliding out of a metal seat. But the little voice in the back of her head told her to accept the chemistry.

"Are we in the clear?" Donovan asked when they stepped onto solid ground.

"Yes." British breathed a sigh of relief.

"Well, well, well."

British cursed under her breath. "Hi, Maggie."

"Hi, British and Hot Guy from the Other Day," said Maggie with a wink. She balanced a round lavender tray of cupcakes as she wagged a finger at Donovan. "I couldn't recall your face the other day at the Cupcakery but I remember you now, Donovan Ravens."

Donovan nodded and extended his hand. "You have me at a disadvantage."

"I'm forgoing lash extensions and makeup, no offense to Ravens Cosmetics." Maggie wiggled her eyebrows, held the tray in one hand above her head and reached in her pocket for her cell phone to pose for a faux selfie, her lips pressed together.

"Magnolia Swayne." Donovan snapped his fingers and pointed. "How are you? What are you doing here? And without your entourage?" He leaned over and gave Maggie a hug.

British bobbed her head between the two of them. Maggie's socialite life had brought her to South Florida for every high-fashion event. It made sense they knew each other.

Another whirlwind from a ride blew a breeze across British's face. Her eyes twitched—correction, just her right eye twitched—as she calculated the distance, arm length and timing of the hug between Donovan and Maggie. She scratched the back of her head and tried to diagnose the sudden irritation rising in her. She liked Maggie. She was the cool big sister of Kenzie. Maggie was also very clear she didn't want a serious relationship, which meant she could be perfect for Donovan. But what did British care?

British cleared her throat. "Well, if you two will excuse me," she began and turned around, right into the six-foot-tall woman who'd given birth to her. "Mom."

"I knew I saw you," exclaimed Joan, who began talking a mile a minute as she wrapped her arms around her daughter's shoulders. The pink-glittered letters of her mother's black, pink and white baseball shirt spelled out Glam-Ma and lit up under the changing lights of the rides behind British. When she pulled back from the hug Joan began wiping the messy glitter off British's cheek. "You haven't answered any of my calls. Where have you been?"

British gently swatted the smothering touch away with the back of her hand. Joan would never change and British loved that about her. She commanded attention, not just because of her stature but because her mother was drop-dead gorgeous, with her short-cropped brown pixie cut that framed her perfectly symmetrical face and bright green eyes. While British had not inherited her mother's height, she did get her light brown skin from her. She hoped when she reached her mother's age her skin would be just as flawless.

"Hey, Mrs. Woodbury," Maggie said, appearing at British's side.

"Dahling," Joan cooed, flashing her pearly white teeth. The pet name was often used when her mother, a former Miss Southwood and Miss Georgia Runner-Up, forgot the other person's name. Maggie lacked makeup, but not that much. "I heard you were in town. Oh? And who is this handsome man escorting you to the fair?"

British prayed the fairgrounds would open up and swallow her whole before she had to listen to her mother flirt. How many times had Joan drilled into British's adult head that she was free to look at the menu? Levi Woodbury felt the same way as his wife and, on the rare occasions British went over to her parents' house for lunch during the day, she caught him catching up on reality shows set on paradise beaches. British's parents recently celebrated their fiftieth wedding anniversary over the summer. They still fawned all over each other and it became worse when all their children came home for the holidays. The bigger the audience, the better.

Maggie pulled Donovan forward and up against British's frame. "No, ma'am, not my date. British's."

"Well," Joan gasped, clutching the pearls around her neck. Only a Glam-Ma wore pearls, a baseball T-shirt, denim and heels to the fair. "I'm British's mother."

"Mrs. Woodbury," Donovan's deep voice greeted her. He stepped closer and his size overpowered British's supersize mother as he took her hand in his. "I see where British gets her beauty from." A kiss to the back of Joan's palm followed the cheesy line.

"Oh please, you got my daughter out and about this time of year—you need to call me Joan." Joan then curtsied. "Sweet Jesus, British baby, is this why you haven't been returning my calls? I completely understand now."

"You called me?" British attempted say with a sincere face but couldn't. She started laughing immediately.

Joan narrowed her dark eyes on British. "So you two are on a date?"

"It's not a date," British explained. "He's staying at Magnolia Palace. We're just friends."

"We're fast friends," Donovan proclaimed along with a slick move: draping his arm around British's shoulder. Maggie made some odd noise between choke and a laugh. Joan made a mewling noise.

"Well, great," Joan said. "In that case, you're coming to Thanksgiving dinner at the Woodburys'."

Back at Magnolia Palace, Donovan and British walked through the quiet foyer. Considering the time the festival had officially shut down, the kids here were probably asleep. Donovan did not recall seeing a teenager running rampant during the last hour he and British had spent with Joan Woodbury. Funny how this weekend he canceled meeting one set of parents and ended up not just meeting a mother but hanging out with her. And he had a blast watching the mother-daughter duo throw darts at balloons, basketball shoot and participate in a water gun race to see who could knock down the most cardboard ducks. No one in the Ravens family would be caught trying fried anything, whether it was a cookie, ice cream or even mystery meat. Joan assured him it was chicken. It felt great being a part of the family, even if it was just her mother. Donovan looked forward to being around the rest of them.

The second hand of the grandfather clock ticked closer to midnight. A glow of a fire roaring in the library fireplace lit the way. A set of parents entering the room nodded in their direction.

As tired as he was, Donovan didn't want his evening to end. He guessed he liked her company so much and the closeness they'd absentmindedly shared, he stretched his long arms out in front of British and reached for the banister. They both touched it at the same time.

Donovan laid his hand on top of hers but she turned to face him on the stairs and let her hand slip to her side. A stab of disappointment hit him. Even two steps ahead of him she was barely at eye level. He could try to kiss her again but hesitated. He didn't want to come off as a douchebag twice in one night. What was he thinking, nearly kissing her on the Ferris wheel when she'd spilled her heart out about her dead husband?

"Hey—" she began.

"Hey—" he said.

She gave a lopsided smile when they both spoke at the same time. With a nod of his head, she continued.

The fire in the library crackled. "Thanks for a great evening," British said.

Donovan cleared his throat. "I need to be the one thanking you. I've been in a rut for the last few days."

"Understandable," she replied. "You broke up with your girlfriend on a soon-to-be aired website footage."

Was she consoling him when she was the one who needed the distraction? She was sweet, but he was ambitious. "If you were aiming to make me feel better, you didn't have to drag me on those death-defying rides."

"Shut up." British giggled and playfully punched him in the shoulder. "They were not that bad."

"My nerves are so frayed I don't think I'll sleep," he teased. "The calmest way to cheer me up would have just been to say yes to me and come work for Ravens Cosmetics."

The next punch landed harder on his arm. "Ow," he said, feigning hurt.

"I have a job," British reminded him. "But I'm glad you had fun."

Donovan nodded. "Yep, and I got an invite to a Thanksgiving dinner. Now maybe my mother will stop calling me. She's freaking out about me not having any stuffing and cranberry sauce."

The bubbly laugh sobered and a soft smile settled on British's face. The flickering fire from the room off to the side highlighted the gold strands in her hair. "You don't have to come. I can make up an excuse."

"What?" Donovan feigned again. "I don't want to disappoint your mom. She loves me."

"Good grief." British rolled her eyes. "I'm not going to be able to stomach the two of you flirting."

"Jealous?"

"Please," she quipped. "I am going to bed."

Donovan took a step closer. He liked the way her eyes widened with surprise. She pressed her hand against his chest to stop him.

"Alone," she clarified with a poke in the chest with her index finger.

"Our rooms are right next door to each other," Donovan explained, grabbing hold of her hand. She didn't pull away, just as she hadn't pulled away when he'd almost kissed her on the Ferris wheel. They paused for a moment. Not wanting to waste another second, Donovan dipped his head lower. British tilted hers to his. And just as he felt the warmth of her breath against his lips, the grandfather clock boldly chimed the midnight hour.

Skittish, British stepped backward up the staircase. "Good night, Donovan."

Not able to move, he nodded his head. "Good night, British. Sweet dreams."

At least waiting for British to disappear from sight gave Donovan a moment to gather himself before being able to walk again. What would she think if she learned he didn't want to walk with her—not out of respect, but to make sure she did not see the raging erection trying to break free? Donovan dragged his hand down his face and whispered a silent prayer to the grandfather clock that had interrupted them. Had it not rung, they might still be on the stairs, tearing each other's clothes off. Maybe, he thought as he climbed the stairs, he needed to curse the clock instead.

In the safety of his bathroom, Donovan turned the cold water on in the walk-in shower. When he realized he'd forgotten his towel, he stepped out of the bathroom, naked. The cell phone on his dresser began to ring.

"Little brother, I hope this is an emergency," Donovan growled when he slid his thumb across Will's face to accept the call.

"Do you ever wear clothes?" Will asked with a disgusted frown on his face.

Donovan flashed his brother the middle finger. He reached for the folded towel at the edge of the bed and wrapped it around his waist. "I'm busy."

"Back to your old habits, huh?" Will laughed. "I'm glad you're done crying and sulking over whatever happened to you. When one girl doesn't work out for you, you always find the next one."

At one point in time, maybe even a week ago, Donovan would have laughed at the comment and taken pride in it. Tonight it seemed more like an insult, as if the only thing Donovan could do was go through women. Right now there was only one woman he wanted. "I don't cry,"

Donovan said, studying the background where Will sat. "Are you in the office working?"

"So?"

"It's after midnight and your hot wife is home alone."

A giggle came over the speaker. "Did he just call me hot?"

A second later Zoe Baldwin Ravens's dark head appeared. Her gold hoops caught the light of the office lamp on Will's desk as she leaned forward.

"Hey, Zoe."

"Hey, Donovan," said Zoe with a welcoming smile. She wiggled her fingers and the Ravens heirloom ring sparkled under the fluorescent office lights. "I'm sorry Will's calling. I stepped out to get us some drinks."

"I'd never blame you," said Donovan. "Everyone in the family already knows Will is crazy."

"Dedicated to the company," Will reminded him. He made room in his chair for Zoe to sit on his lap. Donovan bit back a smile of enjoyment at seeing his brother happy. "Please tell me you're not sleeping with the next potential spokesmodel for RC."

"Not yet," Donovan mumbled. Leaving the phone faceup on his bed, Donovan moved over to the wall he shared with British. The balcony to his room faced the front of the hotel, as did hers. He wondered if she had stepped outside to enjoy the night air.

Will cleared his throat. "We're about to head out of town and we—"

"You," Donovan and Zoe chorused and then chuckled.

"Donovan," Will called out over the line. "I'm serious."

"About what?"

"The perfect woman," Will growled.

"Calm down, sweetie," said Zoe. "Donovan, ignore him. I am sorry we interrupted your evening."

Any other woman, Donovan would have had in his bed by now. British was different. She was special. She was…

Knock, knock, knock. Donovan turned toward the noise at the sliding-glass door to the balcony and found British standing outside.

She was there.

"I gotta go," Donovan said, moving to the bed and switching the phone off with one swipe. Eagerness helped him recross the room. His thumb fumbled with the switch to unlock and pull the door open at the same time. A magnolia scent blew in with a breeze. The trees in the driveway were bare. It had to be her.

"Am I interrupting?" British asked. She bit her lip and shifted nervously back and forth on her bare feet. Instead of the sweater and jeans from earlier, she was wearing a pale blue nightgown. A sweet hourglass silhouette taunted him through the material.

Donovan blinked in disbelief. His throat closed and his body tensed.

British snapped her fingers in his face. "Did I wake you?"

"No." He finally breathed. "Would you like to come in?" Donovan stepped aside but British shook her head.

"No, I won't keep you up."

Too late, Donovan thought, with his erection rising. A towel could only hide so much. For British to not see how immature he was, he leaned forward at an angle and pressed his arm against the jamb. "What's up?"

"I wanted to thank you again for a lovely evening," she said. Her fingers reached for a coil of her hair and twirled it. "And…"

A bit distracted by not seeing the rock on her finger, Donovan shook his head. "And what?" he inquired. If it got any quieter between them, she might be able to hear the pounding of his heart.

"I believe in finishing what I start."

"Which is—?" He barely got his question out before British leaped forward and wrapped her arms around his neck, dragging him to her level. Her soft lips pressed against his. Their mouths opened and tongues discovered each other. She tasted minty and fresh. The warmth of her body scorched his. Bells rang in his head. Never in his life had a kiss from a woman rocked him to his core. He needed more. Donovan let go of the door frame to wrap his arms around her waist, but she pulled away.

"We were interrupted twice," British breathed, "and I don't like going to bed with regrets. Good night, Donovan."

Chapter 6

For the most part, British tried to live without regret, but perhaps she felt a watered-down version of it when she bounced down the steps into the dining room, only to find Donovan seated at the table scanning the front page of the *Southwood Democrat*, the local paper, the following morning. From his profile she noticed he wore a pair of black basketball shorts and a black University of Miami muscle shirt. His arms bulged and British wished she'd worn her hair loose around her face instead of in a bun. Heat crept up from her neck to her ears.

Last night, when he wore nothing but a towel, she'd spotted a tribal half tattoo sleeve over his left shoulder and chest. And here she was, cringing at the flu shot she received last week. The pages crinkled at the fold when he lowered it when she walked into the room. His sideburns rose with the corners of his mouth as he smiled.

"Good morning," he greeted in his deep voice.

Steam rose from the white porcelain cup of black coffee by his side. On the long cherrywood table sat two empty cereal bowls, each one on a place mat on either side of Donovan. The smell of savory bacon filled the air.

"Good morning." British made her way over to the credenza to the wicker bowl of fresh fruit, well aware he was staring at her. As a teacher of middle school kids, British felt it important to be a role model and to dress appropriately for her audience. She wore modest-length pencil skirts and loose-fitting slacks and always paired them with a decent heel and pretty blouse. But away from work, British prided herself on her collection of New Edition T-shirts and jeans. Now she questioned the pink sweats she wore with her white canvas shoes. Anticipating the cooler weather, British also wore a plain white V-necked shirt with a matching zipper hoodie. The kind of women who threw themselves at Donovan were probably six-feet-plus, impeccably dressed women with flawless skin, like her mother.

Damn it, she did not focus on beauty and now here she was, one kiss in and underestimating herself. British palmed an apple and turned to face him, resting her hip on the wooden furniture. "I see the girls have eaten."

"They have," said Donovan. "I sent them to the store to pick up the things they're going to need for their STEM-Off."

"I have an account for them at the hardware store downtown," she said, taking hold of the stem from the fruit. For some reason, she mentally played a juvenile game, twisting the apple in her hand and sounding off the letters of the alphabet. When the stem broke away, the initial landed on would be the person you'd marry. A-B-C-D. *D?* "Seriously?" she mumbled under her breath. This was not what her PhD in STEM Education was about.

"Why spend your own money when I said I'd be a sponsor?"

"Donovan," she said with a warning tone.

"If you agree to being RC's spokesmodel, I believe you can even write it off as a business expense."

"You're incorrigible," she responded.

Donovan lifted a brow over the paper and studied her for a moment. "I didn't hear a 'no' in there."

"Absolutely and unequivocally no, especially not now," British said in a clipped tone.

The gossip column on the front page disappeared as he folded the paper. His thick brows rose in question. "Don't tell me after last night you're changing your mind about me."

To warn him, British glanced in his direction and then darted a glance toward the vacant dining room entrance. She sat down beside him and spoke in a whisper. "The last thing I want is for my students to get the wrong idea."

"That we kissed?"

She hushed him with her furrowed brows and frown. Before she got the chance to scold him verbally, Jessilyn opened the swinging dining room door with her hip. The chef offered British a snarl.

"Here's your breakfast," Jessilyn said to Donovan. She set a bowl and a plate in front of him. While Donovan put the newspaper on the seat beside him, Jessilyn pointed out the items in front of him. "My from-scratch biscuits and a bowl of gravy."

British wanted to be the first to tell Jessilyn how delicious her breakfast smelled but decided not to. The compliment could end up with Jessilyn asking for her to go back into the system and change her grades. But damn, it might be worth it for a biscuit drizzled in the thick, peppery sauce. British's stomach growled.

"Thanks," Donovan said to Jessilyn. "British, I'm sure Jessilyn has more."

"No, thank you," British replied with a sweet smile.

"She's afraid I'll poison hers," explained Jessilyn.

Donovan picked up his fork and knife and cut into the fluffy biscuit, then proceed to dip it into the gravy. British and Jessilyn moved closer to inspect what he was doing.

"Something wrong?" Donovan asked.

"What are you doing to my biscuits?" Jessilyn asked, her arms folded across her chest.

"Eating them?" Donovan responded slowly as if they were the ones who were crazy.

"Why are you dipping your biscuit like a dieter dips her fork into her salad dressing on the side?" British asked.

Donovan sat back in his seat. "This is how eating biscuits and gravy is done."

"By who?" British and Jessilyn asked together.

Ignoring them, Donovan went back to cutting a piece of his biscuit. "This is how we eat them in the South."

"No, honey," snapped Jessilyn. She grabbed the plate from in front of Donovan and slid it, then the bowl, toward British "Ms. B, will you please do the honors?"

"Donovan, you live in South Beach," said British. She picked up the bowl and drizzled the thick, white gravy on top of the partially eaten biscuit. "Here in the true South, we smother our biscuits."

Now satisfied with the proper way the breakfast was being eaten, Jessilyn turned to Donovan, her hands on her hips. "Do you understand?"

"Yes, ma'am," Donovan said, saluting her.

"Fine. I'll bring you another plate."

British devoured his breakfast. She hummed while she chewed. She even contemplated going over to Southwood High School and getting that grade changed. "This is so delicious," British informed Donovan.

"So was the one bite I had." Donovan pressed his elbows on the table and shook his head. "I'm glad my faux pas on biscuits and gravy etiquette created a bond between the two of you. Perhaps now you'll have dinner with me?"

"Donovan," British said, hoping he heard the warning tone in her voice. Her eyes flittered toward the arched entrance where Stephanie's parents giggled and made their way to the table. Apparently the lovefest from last night continued today.

"Yes?" Donovan asked. He smiled devilishly, which only made him more handsome. "Jessilyn wanted to make sure we had a proper dinner tonight before everyone left."

"Everyone's leaving?" British looked up at Stephanie's mother.

"Just for the Thanksgiving break," she told her. "With our house still under construction, we're going to spend the next few days with family in Peachville."

With everyone gone, British realized there'd be no point in her staying, either. Images of her and Donovan rolling around on the king-size bed in his room flooded her mind. Her senses became alert and blood pulsed through her fingertips. British dropped her fork. Everyone at the table stared. "Sorry, y'all. Will you excuse me, please?"

British pushed herself away from the table and briskly walked out of the dining room. This wasn't right. She was here to help the girls with the upcoming competition. If the girls were leaving, there was no point in British staying here. She needed to go upstairs and pack, not to fantasize about the hunk at the end of the table. This couldn't be what Vonna had been talking about when she'd said it was beyond time for British to move on. Tiffani's idea, maybe.

She barely got to the staircase before Donovan caught up with her. His fingers laced around her upper arm as he led her into the library. The blinds were closed tight, sealing out the morning sun. The scent of old books overpowered the faint bacon aroma. British backed up against the wall to the sunroom.

"We always seem to find ourselves in here," Donovan whispered.

"You keep cornering me," said British, squaring her shoulders. The slight movement allowed a sliver of the sun inside the room. Donovan pressed his left hand above the wall just over her head. "You really ought to stop teasing me."

Heart racing, British licked her lips. "I'm sure I don't know what you're talking about. Why do you have me trapped in the library?"

Donovan turned his body to the right and allowed his biceps to point toward the door. "By all means," he teased, licking his bottom lip, "you're free to go, Ms. B."

Maybe it was the pounding in her ears or the distracting way his bulging bicep appeared, but she stayed. "How am I teasing you?"

"First, coming to my room via the balcony last night."

"Yeah…well," British huffed, "it's not like I could knock on your door and risk one of the girls seeing me and get the wrong idea."

"What idea would that be?"

To create space between them, British folded her arms across her chest. "Like I said last night, I didn't want to go to sleep without doing what I wanted to do."

"Which was to kiss me?" Donovan dropped his arm and faced her. "And your point of traipsing into the dining room with your hair like this was?" He reached out and touched a tendril that must have come loose.

British pushed his hand away from her face. The touch sent a shiver down her spine. "Like what?"

"The ole librarian bun at the top of your head."

She blinked blindly.

Donovan's eyes widened. "You don't know about the fantasies men have."

"Considering the librarians I've met…" British began with a deep sigh.

"There was a librarian in college and, if it weren't for her, I probably would never have studied." Donovan closed his eyes long enough for a strange jealous feeling to wash over British. She pushed at Donovan's chest, ignoring the hard muscles of his pecs. His eyes opened and his hand caught her fingertips. She didn't expect to shiver when he brought them to his lips for a soft kiss. "Aw, wait, you can't get mad at me for remembering Ms. Fredd."

"I'm not mad at a thing," British said calmly. Her insides screamed. "I just don't want anyone walking in on us."

"That's good to know." Donovan dropped his left hand and pushed the stray hair behind British's ear.

"What?"

"That you're at least thinking of me and you as an us." He slid his index finger along the slop of her nose.

"Donovan, I…" Again she couldn't find the right words.

"We'll take things slow, British," Donovan said. "And, fortunately for us, we'll be all alone after Thanksgiving."

Slow? Why the hell would she want something slow with Donovan? No, she wanted him fast, hard and sweaty. The back of British's throat went dry. Every image about the two of them together, in each crevice of this hotel, flashed through her mind like 8 mm film.

"Hey, we're back!" Stephanie yelled, coming through the front door. "Mr. D, we even saved you money."

And my hide, British thought to herself. Donovan was in Southwood for one reason only: to get away from his life down south. This made him a perfect choice for her. Eventually he was going to go home and to his life. That's what she wanted. Right?

Later on that evening, Donovan double-checked his garnet-and-gold tie in the mirror behind the vacated concierge's desk. "Don't act like this is your first meal with her, man," he told himself, "other people will be there."

The palms of his hands sweated. His heart raced with anticipation of seeing British again. He rolled his eyes, chiding himself for being so juvenile. Just because he hadn't seen her since breakfast didn't mean he needed to be so nervous. Except he was. Donovan had thrown down the gauntlet. He'd made his intentions clear. *Right?*

Hell, since when did he start doubting himself?

A set of twinkle lights suddenly lit up the hallway, followed by a surprised curse. "Jesus, Mary and Joseph."

"You okay, Mrs. Fitzhugh?" Donovan made his way down the hall to where the housekeeper tried to keep the elevator door open with her foot since her hands were filled with towels. The fresh, clean scent intoxicated him. While the condo in Miami was immaculate, Donovan's housekeeper put everything away herself, including his laundry and dry cleaning. He missed the warm fabric-softener smell from summers with his grandmother. God, when was the last time he'd smelled that scent? Maybe when he was twelve?

"I forgot how smart those girls were," she breathed. "One of them said they wanted to set up a mirror or something so they didn't crash into me."

"Looks like they set up motion sensors," Donovan said with a nod. He looked around to find a plug but figured they were somehow battery-operated. "Genius, I'll have to tell them over dinner tonight."

"Looks like it's just going to be the two of you, love," said Mrs. Fitzhugh.

"What's going on?"

"Didn't you hear about the storm?" The elderly woman began walking toward the hallway. Light flashed through the windows at the end of the corridor.

Since Will left a text every hour on the hour about his deadline, Donovan had turned his phone off. He was still on vacation, damn it. "I smell dinner."

Mrs. Fitzhugh nodded. "That's our little Jessilyn. She's quite the efficient chef. Everything is done." They stopped at a linen closet and she opened the door and pointed. "She finished dinner and headed out early. I hope you don't mind. Mr. Torres said for us to go home for the Thanksgiving break."

Good thing Ramon hadn't mentioned how Donovan had wanted them all to have extra pay for their time, as well, and he'd cover it. Otherwise it might be a bit awkward right now. "Sounds like a great guy," he said.

"He is, and he's even better with the new wife. There's a softer side of him."

Women did that to men. They made them soft. Look at how nervous he was at the thought of seeing British again after eight hours, thirty-three minutes and forty-five seconds. Donovan bent his elbow, twisted his wrist to take a nonchalant glance at his gold watch and tried to ignore the anxious feeling.

Mrs. Fitzhugh chuckled. Her body shook and her cheeks turned red. "You look like you're fighting it."

"Fighting what?"

"The softer side," she explained and then tapped him on the arm. "How long have you been single?"

Donovan flashed the older woman a bright smile. "Are you flirting with me?" He reached out and wrapped his arm around her shoulder.

"Child, I have panties older than you," she said, shrugging him off. "Besides, you're just a boy." Any attempt to get him away from her was feeble. The two of them laughed long and loud. They didn't hear anyone coming. Donovan liked Mrs. Fitzhugh and clearly she did not mind him.

"Be careful there, Mr. Ravens," said a familiar voice at the bottom of the steps. "Mrs. Fitzhugh has a mean right hook. I've seen it."

"Ah, there you are," Mrs. Fitzhugh said soberly, though her face was still red with laughter.

Donovan's heart slammed against his rib cage. British stood there with her arm propped up. She wore a formfitting blue gown that dipped into a V and exposed her full cleavage. Her curly hair hung loose and framed her face.

"I was just informing Mr. Ravens that everyone has taken leave for the night."

British leaned against the banister, almost relieved. "Jessilyn, too?"

"I thought you two bonded over making fun of me?" Donovan asked her.

"Until I change her grade," joked British, "I don't want to be left alone with her."

"But you are eating dinner with us tonight? Right?" Donovan asked eagerly—hopefully not too eagerly. "You're all dressed up."

"So are you," she said, letting her eyes linger up and down his frame. Donovan puffed out his chest.

"Well," Mrs. Fitzhugh said with a nervous headshake, "I'm afraid it's going to be just the two of you for dinner. Everyone else has decided to head on out before the storm hits and the roads get undrivable."

"What about you, Mrs. Fitzhugh?" British asked. "Aren't you going to head out?"

"Oh yes, I don't want to miss Black Friday shopping in town. I wanted to make sure you guys ate."

"Oh please," moaned Donovan. "We can fix ourselves something to eat, can't we, British?"

"I don't know about him, but I can handle the food for everyone."

Mrs. Fitzhugh patted Donovan on the shoulder. "No, when I say everyone else left, everyone left. The van from the Brutti Hotel downtown just picked up a few guests who weren't going to relatives' for tomorrow. It's just the two of you tonight."

Lightning struck again. British reached out and touched Mrs. Fitzhugh's hand. "I think you should stay here instead of trying to make the trip into town."

"Don't be silly. I've got my grandson on the way."

As if on cue, a horn blew outside from beyond the front porch.

"Are you sure? Maybe the two of you can wait out the weather here?" British asked.

Mrs. Fitzhugh shook her head from side to side. "No, best we get on our way before the bottom falls out."

Donovan cocked his head to the side, afraid to ask.

"Before the storm hits."

As the older woman walked toward the door, the last two remaining guests walked with her. She assured them they would be just fine and that British knew every emergency contact in town. They opened the door for her, where her grandson rushed to them with a waiting umbrella. Donovan asked once more if she was okay and before she took off for shelter with her family member, Mrs. Fitzhugh stepped up on her tiptoes and gave him a kiss goodbye.

"Well," British sighed, facing the door as it closed. "What do we do now?"

Donovan loosened his tie and shook his head. "Now we have dessert first."

"What?"

Letting her in on his idea of a treat, Donovan stepped forward and cupped British's face. "Dessert," he whispered before dropping his face to kiss her.

British's arms wrapped around his neck and allowed him to dip her backward. Just as he recalled from last night, the spark was undeniable. British moaned and her lips vibrated against his. His body hardened. To be safe, he set her upright.

"If that was dessert," British asked him, "what's the main course?"

"Well—" he started and stopped himself with her help when she swatted him in the stomach. "All right, all right. But I'm not going to apologize for kissing you just now."

British took a deep breath. "I guess I had it coming."

Donovan narrowed his eyes. "I don't believe my kisses have ever been compared to a form of punishment."

"I didn't mean it to sound like one," said British. "I just meant, if I can just randomly kiss you because I don't want to regret anything, it's only fair you do the same."

A clang of thunder shook the door frame. Donovan laced his fingers with hers and led her to the dining room. This felt natural—as if the two of them just saw off their last guests and were heading upstairs. Only they weren't, Donovan reminded himself. While they'd been sharing a few kisses here and there, Donovan acknowledged the fact that she was a widow. He assumed he was the first person she was attracted to since her husband's death. He needed to keep this in mind. Eventually he was going to leave Southwood. Hopefully it would be with British—as the new spokesmodel for Ravens Cosmetics.

"Well, I figured since we have to be around your family, we need to get this whole sexual tension out of the way."

"You're pretty sure of yourself, Donovan," British said with a nod.

They stopped and stood in the archway of the dining room and faced each other. "I think you wouldn't have showed up in my room in a thin nightgown last night if you weren't feeling the same vibes as me. But I don't want things to get muddled for us. We may end up working together if you take my offer and be Ravens Cosmetics' newest star."

"I won't," she assured him. "Anyway, what are you talking about?" Annoyance dripped from her voice.

It didn't matter to him. She was so adorable, standing there with her hands behind her back, leaning on her side of the arch. "What am I taking things slow with?"

"Well," Donovan began after deeply clearing his throat. "Do we need to have this talk now?"

"Are you referring to me being a widow?" British half laughed. "Are you trying to marry me?"

Donovan felt his eyes widen at the word. "Well... I—"

"Good grief, Donovan," said British. She crossed her arms, tucking her right hand under her arm and her left on top. *Her ringless hand on top.* "I'll admit there is a tension between us. But I can't be sure it's sexual. You've been harassing me about working for your company."

"So when I caught you staring at me this morning?"

She opened her mouth then closed it. "Well, I didn't say you aren't attractive."

"You're turning red, British." He swore if he stepped closer he might spark up in flames.

The light from the candles on the table highlighted her face when she turned away from him. "What you're describing is pure physical desire. Pheromones."

"Oh," he said with a wink, "so animalistic."

"Whatever," she huffed and stepped into the dining room. "It's all science."

"All this science talk," he said rubbing his heart. "You're really turning me on." And she was, but he guessed from the way she rolled her eyes she didn't believe him one bit.

The table was set with antique silver and patterned plates. A silver-domed tray housed a perfectly roasted turkey. Donovan had peeked earlier. British chose a seat by the head of the table, close to where he'd sat this morning. For a moment Donovan pictured three curly-haired kids with features perfectly blending those of the Ravens family and British. He blinked and shook his head. The image disappeared. Weird.

"I see Jessilyn made a turkey," British noted as she started walking toward the French doors. Had they lingered longer, Donovan might have wiped everything off the table and made love to her in front of the turkey. "The sides must be in here," she went on. "How about we just do our dinner buffet-style and save us extra dishes to clean up? Sound good to you? Oh crap."

British rushed through the kitchen where they'd first dined together and headed for the back door. Marker ink drizzled down the white pages of the poster board where steps for the big and small challenges were outlined. Opened plastic coffee filters for the glow-in-the-dark chromatology butterflies took on water. "The girls left some of the equipment you just got them outside and it's raining."

Seemingly without thinking, British kicked out of her heels and jetted out the door. Donovan followed half in fear of making sure she didn't hurt herself and half to do whatever she needed done. "Wait."

Rain poured down between them. He had no idea what half the stuff was but it seemed important. "Load me up," Donovan said, coming up to her.

Without a word she lifted metal rods, batteries, radios and lights into his open arms.

"Correct me if I'm wrong, but is this safe?"

"It's better than wasting the items," British noted, grabbing her own stack and heading for the back porch.

"Yeah, but the items can be replaced," he said. "You can't. And then I'll be forced to find someone else to be RC's spokesmodel." British stopped long enough to give him a pretty snarl. Even soaking wet, he wanted her. But now was not the time.

Donovan followed her movements until they cleaned up the backyard. By the time they finished, the two of them were drenched and found this to be the right time to laugh about it.

"I'm going to have a serious talk with them when they get back," said British. "They can't just waste things. Look at this," she hissed and stepped off the porch. "Stephanie left a controller and her SSRs for her string of lights. The solid state relays are going to connect to the computer, if they're not ruined by now."

What appeared to be a string of loose bulbs turned out to be an underground set that didn't budge. When British bent to pull the lights with a heavy tug, she fell… flat on her back. Donovan darted off the steps to scoop her up. "Are you okay?" he said in a panic. They made it inside before, as Ms. Fitzhugh said, the bottom fell out. Rain fell like a heavy sheet.

"My pride is hurt," said British. "Put me down."

"No way, you're filthy," he said, shaking his head. "If you think I'm a lousy cook, you should see my non-existent housekeeping skills." Donovan hiked British up in his arms for a better grip. "Nope, I'm carrying you to your room."

At least while she pouted she was quiet.

Donovan carried her up the grand staircase and to her closed door.

"Close your eyes," British ordered him. "I'm not hurt."

"Woman, I practically saw your naked tail the other night and if that didn't give me enough view, your split in your dress revealed a whole hell of a lot more."

British did what he expected and rolled her eyes. "Fine, whatever." She reached into the V of her bodice and extracted her card key, giving him an impatient look. Wordlessly she raised an eyebrow and demanded him to lower her enough to unlock the door. Such an easy task to do but so hard for Donovan. He was mesmerized by the swell of her breasts. Rain droplets caressed her skin in places he wished he could.

British cleared her throat and brought him back to focus. "Right, uh, sorry."

Once the door popped open, Donovan set British on the dresser by the door. To silence her from questioning him, he raised his index finger in the air, then went to grab a few towels from the bathroom. By the time he turned back around, British had already slipped the gorgeous gown off her shoulders. She folded her arms across her bare breasts and jutted her chin forward. Donovan shook his head. "Not sorry."

The moment Donovan anticipated for later, started right now. Donovan wedged himself between her wet thighs while he cupped her face. Their tongues reached out for a reunion. British's hands tugged at the knot of his tie and her fingers impatiently ripped open the front of his Oxford shirt. Their feverish kiss didn't break, not even when he led them over to the edge of the bed and coaxed her body backward with his frame. While his left hand held up the lower half of her body, Donovan's hands palmed her breasts. His thumb traced circles on her areolae.

British's hands skillfully worked him out of his wet shirt. He helped with unbuttoning his pants while she slid them over his rear. He wanted her so badly, he barely waited to pull his slacks completely off. He fumbled in the dark with the condom in his wallet, hating himself for taking too much time away from devouring her body.

British waited with her elbows up and legs open. The color of her dress on the floor caught the flickering light of the sky outside. Keeping them safe, Donovan felt his way up her calves, to her muscled thighs and to the apex of her legs. His fingers pushed at the fleshy wet center, his erection straining against the rubber material.

British sat up enough to grab Donovan by the neck and pull him down into a warm kiss. While he pressed her body onto the bed, he entered her slowly. British pressed her body against his. Her breasts crushed against his chest and her legs wrapped around his waist. Donovan wanted to take it slow but as she nibbled his ear he lost himself in her and brought her to the first of many more orgasms that were sure to come.

From the moment their bodies connected, British knew there was something irreversible between her and Donovan. A part of her wanted to feel guilty for being with another man but her heart wouldn't let her. This felt right. His body was so hard with muscles and had been so strong to have lifted and carried her earlier this evening; his skin was so soft. Donovan turned onto his belly and British stroked his bare back.

Donovan turned his face toward her. His smile melted her heart. "Are you okay?" he asked, reaching over to stroke her face. The pad of his thumb brushed just beneath her lower lashes.

"I'm fine," she answered with a soft smile, "everything is fine."

"I don't want you to have any regrets," said Donovan.

British turned her face to kiss the inside of his palm. Her lips twitched with a grin as he shivered. "I'm where I want to be, doing what I want to do." She leaned over and kissed Donovan on the lips. With gentle aggression she coaxed his mouth open and tasted him again. Reenergized, she pushed her body against his to urge him on his back. "I don't think I can get enough of you."

Donovan obliged and held on to British's hips while she straddled his naked waist. Her body urged him to flip on his back. His hands reached for her breasts and held them, kneading them gently. Electricity bolted through her body. She realized a difference between being with Christian and being with Donovan. Donovan didn't tire. His erection pulsed between her legs. British nibbled her bottom lip, contemplating what to do next or where to start. She wasn't used to this wanton behavior but she wanted to devour Donovan.

Donovan sat up with her in his lap and whispered the words that filled her heart with joy and security. "We can take our time. I'm not going anywhere."

Chapter 7

A harsh, old-fashioned-sounding bell went off next to British's ear. She stirred in her bed and reached aimlessly to stop the sound. Blindly she found the alarm clock and hit a button to get the noise to stop. British shuddered. Her body naturally sought the heat source in her bed and found it in an oversize man. Not just any man. Donovan Ravens. She smiled as she blinked her gaze into focus. His broad back faced her. The tips of her fingers itched to trace the tattoo on his body, but she decided to wait. There was something else she needed to do but, as she lifted the covers for a peek at his bare butt, she forgot what it was.

"Dear God, woman," Donovan croaked, "are you ready to go again?"

Giggling, British lifted herself up on her right elbow. What she'd thought was her room was actually his. That's right. She'd followed him in here through the balcony when he'd left to get more condoms for the two of them and they'd ended up christening the room in here. "I forgot, you're an old man."

The little bit of covers she still wore left her body. Donovan rolled toward her, taking the blanket but replacing it with his strong arms. She'd take those any day. Last night with Donovan...this morning with Donovan, had been incredible. All she needed to do was to think about the things he did to her and she was ready to go.

"I'm old, huh?" Donovan flicked both nipples with his tongue.

A spark of desire pumped through her. "I don't recall those exact words."

Donovan ducked his head under the sheets. His full lips started a trail of kisses down her diaphragm across her belly. She was suddenly self-conscious of how desperately she needed to clean up. British pulled him back by his massive shoulders. "I need to shower, I must smell horrific."

"Let's shower after we lie here for a while," said Donovan and closed his eyes. He pulled himself back up to the pillow by hers and, without thinking, British cocked her leg over his. They just fit together.

The realization came that she'd just been intimate with another man after a long...long time. British didn't want to compare the two men but it was inevitable. She and Christian learned to make love together. The men were different. Christian, because of his heart, had to limit his overexcitement. British felt a mix of exhilaration and fright at Donovan's uninhibited passion. She'd assumed Donovan would be a great lover physically, but mentally he went beyond her expectations. He anticipated needs she didn't know she had. Donovan paid attention to every inch of her body, from her toes to the top of her head. Euphoria settled into her veins. Not wanting to forget this feeling, British rested her head but didn't close her eyes. At least, she didn't think she had shut them until a loud shrill woke her. This time it wasn't the alarm clock. It sounded like a doorbell.

"I thought we were alone," said British.

"Hell, I paid for everyone to stay away," Donovan growled and stalked naked toward the balcony door, which faced the front entrance of Magnolia Palace.

Damn, the man looked good naked. The white curtains billowed in the cool fall breeze. A faint smell of burning wood from a smoker on a nearby estate filled the bedroom.

A voice called out from the front lot, "British, honey," and broke the silence of the morning.

British flopped back onto the bed. "Please tell me..."

Donovan half turned to catch what she was going to say. She wanted the bed to swallow her whole. "Is that...?"

"British, it's your mom. Come let me in. I'm worried. You haven't picked up and you know I like to start cooking first thing in the morning."

The alarm clock on the side of Donovan's bed went off again. This time British turned it off and remembered what today was. Thanksgiving.

Not since before his accident did Donovan recall a time he felt the panic need to leap out of bed, but that's what he'd done when he heard British's mother was downstairs waiting for them to make sure they came over to the house. Donovan would have preferred spending the day in bed with British, especially after last night and this morning—and even more when they stopped in the driveway to British's family home.

"Well, there's my little girl."

Donovan hung back by the car when a burly, oversize man stepped out of the two-story farmhouse with a shotgun by his side. Folks were serious about their guns in the South. The summer Will and Zoe met, Will had been cleaning weapons with one of Zoe's friend's husbands when a young man came to the house to pick up the teenager for a date. Somehow Donovan knew this was no act. This was British's father. He stood there dressed in dark green camouflage and large rubber boots, holding a long rifle.

When Joan corralled them this morning, she promised Donovan she'd take good care of him once they got to the house. Before Donovan closed the passenger-side door for British, she'd already high-stepped it around his car. He tried not to stare at her hourglass figure in her formfitting jeans. The baseball T-shirt she wore with the red sleeves accentuated the curves of her rounded breasts. He couldn't believe that less than an hour ago he was holding her in his bed and now here he was, with her family, all vulnerable. He took a deep breath of the cool morning air and pushed the thoughts out of his head. Three months ago, before Tracy, women had rotated in and out of his life. There'd barely been time for name exchanges, let alone hanging out with the parents. Yet somehow with British, this just felt natural. He liked her and enjoyed being around her.

Joan pulled her red SUV into the winding redbrick driveway right behind Donovan, leaving him to wonder if this was a trap. If Joan had figured out what was going on this morning, she hadn't let on when they'd met her downstairs in the lobby.

"Hey, Daddy." British walked across the manicured lawn and maneuvered her way through the already-placed Christmas decorations. "What do you have going on here? I thought the Christmas Council said no decorations are supposed to be put up before Thanksgiving."

A twinge of guilt hit Donovan. He kicked the toe of his Timberlands against the bottom of the car to get any dirt off and to distract himself for a moment. He wondered what his brothers were doing right about now. Will said he and Zoe were heading out of town, which seemed like an odd thing to do this time of year but maybe that was marriage and the two wanted to be alone. Donovan understood. He preferred to stay in on the traditional family holiday instead of being pecked with questions from his sisters about Tracy's absence or worse, whether Donovan had made any headway on finding a new spokesmodel for RC.

His family gathered every year at his grandmother Naomi's compound for an old-fashioned, catered Thanksgiving. Given that Naomi had spent her whole life cultivating the company, learning how to cook was never one of her strong suits. No one in his family had learned how… Well, the twins, Dana and Eva, had learned once they married. Maybe later he'd give them a call. The caterers usually left around four in the afternoon. Making a mental note, Donovan took a deep breath.

"Thanksgiving started at midnight," said her father, wagging his finger at his daughter. They met at the bottom step and he pulled her into a big bear hug, twirling her around in the air. Like her mother, British's father was equally tall. "Who's this?"

"This is Donovan," said British.

At the exact moment British turned to face him, Donovan blew out his held breath. How was she going to describe him? What were they? Why did he care? He didn't believe in labels. Usually it took him weeks to figure out what category to place women. They never made it to girlfriend status, though the media may have suggested different.

"Donovan," British went on, "this is my dad, Levi Woodbury."

"I already told you," Joan told her husband with a huff and a wink at Donovan.

"Ah, yes, I remember now." Levi Woodbury stepped forward and extended his beefy hand. "Pleased to meet you, son. Welcome to Thanksgiving at the Woodburys'."

"Wait," a little voice said from the wooden door with the stained glass window, "so we have another member for the football game?"

British leaned at the waist. "Eli? Is that you or a grown man?"

A little kid fully emerged onto the porch in a pair of superhero turtle pajamas. In a while, British managed to greet a half dozen or so nieces and nephews, who all surrounded her like she was a celebrity. Their screaming brought out British's siblings and, one by one, Donovan met her family.

"Donovan, this is my brother Finn, my sister Cree, and twin sister and brother, Irish and Scots."

Donovan tried to remember everyone's name. They all favored each other and shared a blend of their parents' looks. The two sisters favored British with their curly hair but their attitudes were completely different. One of them seemed to *mother* British while the other *smothered* her. Both ladies fussed over British's hair to the point where she ended up tying it in a bun at the top of her head, which only got them talking about her denim leggings and green Converse shoes not being representable.

"Leave my baby alone," Levi spoke up. "She's dressed just fine. They were fourteen and fifteen when British came along so as you can see, they like to pretend she's theirs."

"Thanks, Daddy." The rest of the Woodbury family rolled their eyes.

"Donovan—" Levi turned his attention from his kids "—you look to be in good shape."

"I try, sir."

"Great, we're waiting for the turkey to get done but in the meantime the rest of us are going to play some football," said Levi. "My crybaby boys have been complaining about being on my team."

Scots stepped forward with his hands in the air. "You see that, man?" he said to Donovan. "My pops doesn't know how to throw yet he insists on playing quarterback. See my hand? See my crooked fingers?" Scots thrust his fingers in Donovan's face.

"You're supposed to catch with your hands like this." Their father demonstrated the proper way for everyone. "Are you a crier?" Levi asked Donovan.

"He doesn't cry." British's declaration might have signed Donovan's death warrant.

Given the size of Levi, Donovan understood why the man wanted to play. However, the evidence staring him in the face gave him pause. Thankfully, Finn stepped forward. Like his father, he was dressed in a pair of green camouflage overalls. "We're going huntin', Pop."

Relieved, Donovan's shoulders dropped. "Aw, man."

"Don't listen to them," Joan said. "No one is going anywhere."

The men and boys, including Levi, all sighed with disappointment, not that Joan seemed to care. She kept walking up the porch steps. "The turkey is not the only thing that's not ready. I need some help in the kitchen. Donovan?"

Donovan smiled apologetically at the group. "Sorry,

but if the food is going to taste as good as it smells now, I've got to go with her."

"Smart friend you have here," Cree said, linking her arm through Donovan's.

"Yeah, British," Irish chimed in. "Where have you been hiding him?"

"I," British declared, "haven't been hiding him anywhere. He's been hanging out at Magnolia Palace."

Donovan heard the catty tone between the sisters. He waited for British to claim him...yet he still didn't know why. He'd known women a lot longer than he had her and cared less what they thought of him.

The inside of the Woodburys' home was not as Christmassy as the outside. A bare tree stood in the corner of the living room to the right. Two women were cleaning off the mantel, placing pictures in a box. Donovan wished he'd seen them. What had British looked like as a child? He pegged her as a tomboy wearing overalls, hunting gear and pigtails. The ladies stopped what they were doing to come and greet the two of them. They each hugged British and introduced themselves to Donovan as the wives of Scots and Finn. Jenny and Scots had been married for ten years, Nicole and Finn fifteen. Two gentlemen came downstairs, complaining about being abandoned in the attic, but stopped once they saw their young sister-in-law. British hugged them and introduced Cree's and Irish's husbands, Tom and Robert.

A long table with a fall-themed tablecloth stood in the center of the dining room with a table setting for sixteen.

Joan led them through the dining room into the kitchen with a long bar. Beyond the bar sat a breakfast nook with a table filled with coloring books and crayons. Covered dishes lined the bar. Pots and pans boiled on the flat-topped stove and when Joan leaned over to open the crowded oven, the savory smell of roasting turkey filled the air. Donovan's stomach growled.

"We have been nibbling all morning," Joan said to him. She pointed at the credenza in the open space of the family room with different levels of brunch foods ranging from a stack of pancakes, sausage and bacon to waffles and eggs under a clear dome.

The Macy's Thanksgiving Day Parade played on the wide-screen television mounted on the wall in front of an L-shaped gray couch. A set of matching gray love seats sat against the half wall that led to a staircase to the second floor. An oversize fir tree stood on the opposite side of the room by the sliding-glass doors.

"We're starving," said British, taking hold of Donovan's elbow.

"'We'?" Cree picked up on her sister's choice of words.

British glared at her before grabbing a silver-trimmed plate. "Yes 'we.'"

"Donovan…" began Joan. "We know British has been staying at Magnolia Palace with the STEM girls. Have they been bothering your stay in Southwood?"

Donovan accepted a plate from British. "I wouldn't say bothering me."

"Please, he's practically a member of the team by now," British groaned. They stood side by side in front of the food and when she looked up at him, she winked.

Returning the wink, Donovan bumped her shoulder. "We're thinking about changing it to Guys Raised in the South, huh?"

Before laughing, British rolled her eyes. "How many times do I have to tell you, Miami is not the South?"

"You're from Miami?" Joan asked him as she straightened the tablecloth.

"Yes, ma'am," answered Donovan.

The other Woodbury men came into the kitchen and began quickly snacking and grabbing cookies from a Christmas-tree-shaped, tiered metal tray by the double-door refrigerator. "Stop it," said Joan, shaking a crayon at them. "You'll ruin your meal."

"This meal is taking forever," said Scots. His wife, Jenny, joined his side and took the cookie away from him.

Donovan fiddled with the plate in his hand and smiled. He missed his family.

"The new guy gets to eat," Finn pointed out.

"His name is Donovan," Joan clarified, "and he's a guest in this home. Next Thanksgiving, he won't get the same treatment."

Something about the idea of a return to Southwood filled Donovan with something…good. It wasn't like he hadn't been around family before. In fact, British's family structure resembled Donovan's, including the constant bantering. When his cousins and siblings joked around, their banter always dealt with the family business. Donovan cocked his head to the side and recalled that most of their exchanges surrounded who did better in their field or who was responsible for sales. British's family was more relaxed. They teased British about her failed science experiments that had led to the kitchen being remodeled twice. It was clear everyone in British's family was proud of her. Donovan could get used to this atmosphere.

"Great, more hands to help decorate at midnight," Scots said. "I'm ready for a nap."

"So we're not going hunting tonight?" Finn spoke up.

British slid into her seat at the nook. "If you're going hunting, does this mean Black Friday shopping is out tomorrow?"

"Black Friday shopping?" Donovan pierced his sausage link with a fork and perked up. "I want to go."

"No," said British.

"C'mon." Joan beamed. "British, mind your manners. Donovan, would you like to go with us tomorrow?"

"I'd love to. I've never been."

British bowed her head. The sisters-in-law dropped their tinsel, the sisters wavered in near-faints, and all of the Woodbury men and in-laws wiped their hands down their faces. Donovan chuckled at everyone's reactions. He felt the need to explain. "With my schedule, I usually shop online for everyone."

"You have no idea what you've just done," British said under her breath.

Donovan shrugged his shoulders. "What? I'm looking forward to this."

"We wake up at three," said Irish. She took a seat across from the two of them and propped her elbows on the table. A few strands of gray stretched through her curly brown hair, which she kept in a side bun. Donovan couldn't guess her exact age, but she aged beautifully. "What do you do for a living, Donovan?"

"He works for his family's company," British supplied. "He's in finance."

"Oh, you must love math," Irish said, sitting back. "The two of you must have a lot in common."

Cree came over and joined them with two glass mason jars of tea. Like her sister, the only way Donovan could tell she was of a certain age was by the gray in her hair and the slight crinkles at the corners of her eyes when she smiled, which she did every time she looked at her baby sister.

"Donovan," Cree said, "do you recall your first words, or at least what your parents said?"

British dropped her fork. "Seriously, Cree? Mom," she whined.

"Cree, leave your sister to her friend."

Ignoring the warning, Cree, thankfully, continued. "We all knew British was going to be smart because her first words weren't anything like 'mama' or 'daddy.'"

"Or 'sister,'" Irish interjected, "as in the sister who stayed up with her so the old no-business-having-kids-after-forty could get rest."

A deep belly laugh filled the kitchen. Levi wrapped his arms around his wife's waist and dipped her back for a kiss—but not before making a statement to make all of the other adults groan. "We're still trying."

"Every single night," Joan gloated.

British was the first to recuperate. Her eyes were still wide and cheeks beet red. "You see why I didn't want you to meet my parents?"

"They're cute," said Donovan. They certainly were different from his parents, Mark and Evelyn Ravens. It wasn't like Donovan grew up in a strict household, just a busy, business-oriented one. The company came first. Yes, the family spent time together but most of it was at the corporate office in Miami. Donovan's parents provided the best for their children and he appreciated the things he was given. It was just different here, warmer almost. His parents touched when they posed for cameras at functions. British's parents touched each other, a lot, whether with a pat on the back, a brush against each other's shoulders or even a flat-out kiss. This was better. "I want to be like that one day."

"Married?" British's eyebrows went up. She bumped his shoulder again, seemingly intent on teasing him.

The notion suddenly didn't seem so frightening. "Yes," he responded honestly.

"On behalf of my brothers and sisters, I apologize for our parents' behavior," said Cree.

"Whatever," groaned Irish. "We only have to worry when Daddy starts talking in his accents."

Everyone started to laugh and even though Donovan had no idea what was going on, he laughed, too. The rest of the morning melted into the noon hour. Donovan helped in the kitchen for a while. He sliced through hard-boiled eggs, whipped up the cream for the dessert later and stirred the greens several times. While the turkey finished up in the oven, Levi wanted to get out in the yard with his new partner. The football game consisted of Donovan, the brothers-in-law and Levi on one team versus the other Woodburys. Donovan's team won but Cree's husband, Tom, got hurt in a tackle…by his wife.

Joan declared the home football game over and invited everyone inside for dinner. Once the meal was blessed, dishes began being passed around. Donovan stuffed himself on dressing, collard greens, sweet potato soufflé for dessert, turkey and ham. He paced himself to make room for the baked goods. All types of desserts sat on the credenza where breakfast had been served and included apple pie, sweet potato pie, dark chocolate cake and a yellow cake slathered in chocolate icing by British's four nieces. Since Cree lived up north with her husband, someone had made a pumpkin pie and sat it down next to the sweet potato one. Donovan impressed the family with his knowledge of the difference between the orange pies.

Once they loaded the dishwasher after the meal, everyone settled down into the family room to watch football. Cree and her husband went upstairs. The half dozen nieces wanted British to read them a bedtime story and Donovan did not mind hanging out with the rest of the Woodburys. He sat on the edge of the couch and rooted for the Dallas Cowboys; they had recorded the Dallas game earlier so they could finish watching the Detroit one after the family football match. Donovan was in his element. It felt great to relax around these people he just met today. They brought him into the fold and Donovan felt like one of the Woodburys and couldn't wait to do this for the next holiday. The thought made him sit up.

"Hey, Donovan," Irish whispered from her seat in one of the chairs by the stairs.

Donovan turned his gaze away from the television. Irish thumbed through one of the boxes with Christmas items at the side of the chair. "Hi, Irish."

"In case you haven't realized, we're all happy to have you here this evening."

"I'm grateful for you all inviting me into your home and taking me under your wing," Donovan replied. Their maternal grandmother, who had arrived just before the meal, seemed to approve, as well. At least, he thought so, if there was any indication coming from the way Joan's mother clung to his arm the entire meal. British had found it embarrassing but Donovan had not. She was pushing one hundred, but Donovan saw clearly that Joan's genes had started with her. Impressive to sit at a table with four generations of beauty.

Robert, Irish's husband, cleared his throat when he came into the family room with a plate of apple pie. "It took having our third child before I was allowed to help with dinner."

"And after that you were banned," Finn stated.

Levi snorted in his sleep.

"Well, I am glad to see British happy," said Irish.

"I am not sure it's my doing," Donovan replied. "But I do know she's fun to be around."

Scots stretched his legs across his wife's in the love seat. "Exactly how much time are you planning on spending with our little sister? Ouch," he cried out when his hair was pulled. "What?"

"I get it," Donovan chuckled. "I have sisters, too."

"Well, how long do you plan on staying in town, Mr. Ravens?" Joan asked. "Aren't they missing you at Ravens Cosmetics?"

Identity exposed, Donovan widened his eyes. "I did not mean to omit anything."

"You didn't, not really. I used to model," said Joan. "I did a few print ads for your grandmother—pre-children, of course."

"I would have said recently," Donovan answered honestly. British's mother blushed the same way British did. "To answer your question, I am on a hiatus right now. I can go back whenever. Right now, though, I am dying to see the STEM-Off go through."

"If British is letting you get involved with the GRITS team, you must be pretty special," said Irish. She fiddled with the items in a box. "You are aware of Christian, right?"

"I am. He sounded like a wonderful man."

Everyone agreed.

"I am impressed British let you help with the girls," said Finn. "After Christian died, British put all her energy and dedication into her work and teaching STEM to the girls, even if she had to do it at that youth center."

"And the insurance money Christian left her," added Scots. "Don't forget that."

"Burns my ass the way she's been frozen out by the science department," said Finn.

This burst of information piqued Donovan's interest. The idea of someone not treating British fairly didn't sit right with him. He balled his fists against his thighs. He needed names and he needed them now.

"Oh, look," Irish cooed, "here's a photo of British." She leaned across the distance and handed Donovan an old photograph. Out the corner of his eye he caught British coming down the stairs, but her movements seemed to happen in slow motion.

"No-no-no-no-no," British repeated. But it was too late. She arrived at the arm of the couch with her hands over her face.

"British," Donovan said, standing. In confusion, he shook his head. She lied. Why would she lie after everything they'd talked about? "All this time you've been shooting me down about being the spokesmodel for Ravens Cosmetics, making it seem the job was beneath you?" The initial knee-jerk reaction was anger but compassion struck him as soon as he saw the pain in British's face.

"You were offered a job to be their spokesmodel?" Joan asked, standing, as well.

British rolled her eyes at her mother and huffed, "I'm not that person anymore."

"Once a beauty queen, always a beauty queen," Donovan told her. "You're perfect."

"Yeah…well, it's hard to imagine I'm perfect when the whole reason Christian is dead is because of me and my stupid beauty queen obligations."

So many questions entered Donovan's mind. Why or how did she think she was responsible for her husband's death? The quiver in British's voice broke Donovan. All he wanted to do was hold her until all her pain went away. He felt helpless for not knowing what to say or do. "Oh, British," everyone in the room chorused.

Tears welled in British's eyes. Donovan felt like a jerk, especially when she stormed outside through the sliding-glass door.

Chapter 8

A fall breeze blew leaves on top of the aqua-blue water of the pool next to her parents' deck. British shivered against the back of the blue-and-white Adirondack chair she sulked in. There was always a reason why she didn't want to come home for the holidays. Her parents and siblings made too much of a big deal about British not seeing professional help after Christian passed away. She accepted his death, knew she was widowed and subconsciously believed his death was her fault. At the time of his death British still volunteered in pageantry. Her intent was to encourage young beauty queens to reach for more than a title and break the glass ceilings in the scientific fields.

Five years ago, however, British forgot her crown at home. It was easier to hold everyone's attention if British wore her tiara and her lab coat. Christian offered to drive home and get it, which he did. Christian swerved to avoid hitting it and ran into a tree. Her tiara was found on the seat of the passenger's seat when a deer ran across the road. She guessed this holiday weekend exposed her suppressed thoughts and had manifested when Irish brought out the old photograph. Maybe she overacted.

The first year without Christian, everyone had stepped on eggshells not to mention his name. They'd taken down the wedding photographs, like she didn't have any at her apartment. But then tonight, to bring up the pageantry to Donovan? *Ugh*, she groaned inwardly. Had she not overheard part of the conversation while she'd finished the bedtime stories upstairs, there'd be no telling what other things Irish would have spilled. British argued with herself, shaking her head. She should have never agreed to come over.

"You're going to freeze out here."

British glanced over her shoulder and rolled her eyes toward the water when she saw her mother coming with a dark plaid blanket. The temperature had been dropping all day. Steam rose from the hot tub at the end of the porch near the bricked-in grill. Orange glows of backyard bonfires shone in their nearest neighbors' yard.

"Not only did I give you life, but I'm bringing you warmth, too, and you're going to sit up here and roll your eyes at me?" Joan tossed the wool blanket over British's shoulders and took a seat on a matching chair to face her.

"I didn't roll my eyes," British lied. She adjusted the blanket to fit her shoulders evenly and stretched her legs out in front of her.

Joan sat in the same position as her daughter. "You forget I raised you."

"Tell that to some of my brothers and sisters in

there." British pointed her thumb at the sliding-glass door. They'd undermined her at every corner today, from cooking in the kitchen to dessert. They'd mocked her for using science to help cook and had had the nerve to bring up all her embarrassing childhood stories, including her time as a beauty queen.

"They love you."

"You mean to make fun of me," British huffed.

"You do understand this is the first time they've been able to experience this with you?"

"Experience what?" British asked, sitting up. "They never acted like that with Christian."

Joan sat up, as well. She reached over and patted British's leggings-clad leg. "Dear, you and Christian grew up together. He and his family ate at our Thanksgiving table all throughout high school. Finn, Cree, Irish and Scots always saw Christian as part of the family. Seeing you with another man…"

"I'm not with another man," British lied again. Her spine tingled, reminding her just how much she *had* been with him last night. It was all she could do to keep from combusting each time she bumped an arm against his in the house—her soul caught on fire.

"Again," Joan sighed, "why are you trying to lie to me? Or are you trying to convince yourself there's nothing between you and Donovan Ravens?"

British shrugged her shoulders.

"Donovan is the first man you've brought home."

"You invited him," British reminded her.

Joan chuckled. "Girl, I am not going back and forth with you about this. It is evident there's something going on between the two of you and I don't want to have to tell you what my intuition is telling me."

British turned to face her mother and contemplated

testing out what she thought was going on. Did she want to tell her that for one moment in her life she wanted to have a quick fling with no attachments and that Donovan was the perfect person for the job?

"Mom."

"You're twenty-eight," Joan went on. "Not dead."

"You sound like Vonna."

"Your mother-in-law is right. Hell, at seventy, your dad and I are still very—"

"All right, we're done here." British got to her feet. Her hands flew up to cover her ears as she focused on the rippling water of the pool. Suddenly her eyes focused on a pair of bathing suits by the Jacuzzi. Since no one else lived here during the year, the garments could only belong to her parents. British frowned.

Joan stood behind British and wrapped her arms around her shoulders. "Sweetie, no matter what's going on in here—" she tapped British's temple "—or here—" and tapped her heart "—I love you."

"Thanks, Mom." British stared off into the horizon.

"And, dear…" she whispered. "Dessert's here."

Raising her brows, British shook her head. "We had dessert."

Gently, Joan spun British around by the shoulders. British looked beyond her mother's height to find Donovan standing outside by the chair she'd just vacated. He wore his khaki chinos and someone else's black hoodie, zipped to his neck. In his hand he balanced a round tray with two…cupcakes.

"I'll leave you two alone," Joan whispered.

Donovan smiled, mouthed a thank-you to Joan and leaned down to kiss her on the cheek. British's heart ached. Christian used to do the same thing. Her mother was right. Christian had been a big part of the family for so long. Maybe it was wrong for her to allow Donovan to come. Yet, here she was staring at him and feeling differently than ever before in her life.

"Hi." Donovan stepped closer.

"Hey," she replied. This was the first real moment they'd had alone since this morning, which seemed so long ago. "What do you have there?"

"Something called the Blues Be Gone cupcake," Donovan replied. "They arrived while you were out here."

British's eyes widened. She craned her neck to the side and spotted Vonna and Tiffani quickly turn around as if they weren't spying on them. She wasn't surprised to see them here. They were close with her family and had probably finished up their Thanksgiving dinner and came out to visit. "That's my mother-in-law," she explained to him as she shook her head. "Or is it former?"

"She's family," Donovan answered.

"Donovan, I—I—" she stuttered and tried to find the words.

"Let me say this," he said. "I want to apologize if I made you feel pressured about coming to work for my family's company, especially not knowing what I do now."

"Thanks," British half-heartedly said.

"But you have to know that the car accident wasn't your fault."

Now with her shoulders squared, British sighed. "Why? Because that's what Irish told you?"

"Not just Irish," Donovan admitted with a nod. He set the tray of cupcakes down on the table between the chairs and stepped closer. "Finn, Scots and Cree came downstairs to tell me about the accident."

"They had no right."

"The accident happened," said Donovan. "It was this time of year. Your dad says deer season runs this time of year and the animals are prevalent in this area. It's not fair, but these things happen."

"Christian wouldn't have been on the road if I didn't forget my tiara for my motivational talk at a beauty pageant," British argued, but didn't put up a fight when Donovan wrapped his arms around her waist and pulled her close, tucking himself in the plaid blanket, as well.

"According to your mother-in-law, Christian was born with cardiomyopathy and lived longer than ever expected and she says it was because of you."

British's head moved to the side, catching Vonna blatantly staring at them, even giving British the thumbs-up of approval before closing the curtains. "She's crazy."

"And insistent," Donovan added. "She said we need to eat these cupcakes right now." He moved away to grab one of the desserts. "You have a wonderful family, British. Thank you for inviting me."

I didn't, she opened her mouth to say, but received a mouthful of frosting.

"Try the cake, British," Donovan teased. He wiped his finger across her upper lip to get the rich icing.

"I'm going to kill my family for their big ole mouths."

Not satisfied with the job his finger did, Donovan lowered his mouth to hers and used his tongue to clean her lips, nibbling for a moment on her bottom one. "Don't kill them just yet. I have been recruited to play Santa in the winter festival on Saturday."

Saturday, she thought, her pulse starting to throb wickedly. "Well, aren't we becoming domesticated?"

"Hell, I don't mind," Donovan chuckled. "I'll learn how to cook and clean better for all this good food I've been eating. I swear I gained ten pounds today."

"I guarantee you'll work it off tomorrow if you're still up for Black Friday shopping."

Donovan took a step back to grandstand his opportunity to unzip the gray sweatshirt. He revealed her mother's latest design of family T-shirts. This one was a Christmas-green, cotton, long-sleeved T-shirt with #TeamBlackFriday across the front with a set of cartoonish elves at the bottom of the hashtagged word.

"Dear Lord," British gasped and took a bite of her cupcake while her eyes rolled back in ecstasy. She savored the sweet potato flavor with the bourbon maple-bacon frosting.

"Oh wait—" Donovan turned around "—it gets better." He stripped out of the black hoodie and tossed it to the side, turning his back to her.

Like any regular hot-blooded American woman, British was a bit distracted by the sight of Donovan's rear in his jeans and bowed legs.

"What do you think?" Donovan asked.

"Oh yeah." She laughed at the shirt. The writing—If Lost, Return to This Lady—was typical Joan, along with an oversize picture of her mother's face. "You have no idea what you're in for tomorrow."

Donovan clapped his hands together. "Speaking of tomorrow. I've got some good news."

"What's that?" British perked up.

"Right after giving me this shirt and before I came out here to talk to you, your mom said I could spend the night."

British did a quick calculation of the six bedrooms they already had and the fact that her room was where the little kids were sleeping. Donovan would probably take the couch in the downstairs family room. She'd have to cross where her parents slept in order to get to where they'd put Donovan. She tried to weigh out her options and routes.

Reading her mind, he shook his head back and forth. "You're really trying to get me killed today," Donovan laughed. "We've got all the time in the world, sweetheart."

Except they didn't. Donovan's vacation had to end eventually.

"The building looks recently renovated," Donovan said, taking hold of British's keys to her apartment in downtown Southwood after a long and tiring day of Black Friday shopping. "Have you lived here long?"

They'd woken before dawn and hit the sales immediately, driving over to the malls in Peachville and Samaritan, and finishing up at the boutiques in Southwood. They'd headed back to the Woodburys' for leftovers and dessert before dark if they got hungry. The only thing British had a taste for right now was Donovan. It took her forever to fall asleep last night. Knowing Donovan slept one floor below on the couch teased her light dreams with the things they could do. She'd replayed every way in her mind she could get to him, including him sneaking up to her room or climbing down the trellis of her childhood bedroom window.

It was weird having a man let himself into her apartment, but at the same time, not. After spending the last forty-eight hours with Donovan, he'd become almost a part of her. British lifted the straps of her purse off her shoulder and set it on the Victorian chair by the front door, which immediately opened into the neat living room with the Victorian floral couch facing them. Lesson plans cluttered the glass coffee table. The bookshelves were mingled with photographs of classrooms and after-school accomplishments. She wondered if Donovan expected to see a shrine to Christian.

"I moved in about four and a half years ago after Christian died." Without looking at him, she knew Donovan quickly calculated the timing of everything. She kicked out of her canvas sneakers and pushed them against the shoe rack by the door. "I lived with my parents the first six months after the funeral."

"Only six?" His voice hinted at humor.

"You've met my parents," British said with a laugh. She watched Donovan stroll into the living room with his hands clasped behind his back, inspecting all the photographs and then the view from the balcony. He wore a pair of fitted denim jeans and a long-sleeved, hunter green Henley shirt that he'd picked up while shopping today. Since Thursday morning he hadn't shaved. The beard he sported had thickened. The rugged look was rather sexy. He turned with a questioning stare.

"There's only so much a grown woman can handle living under the roof of her parents," she went on to explain, "but the deciding factor was listening to my dad speak with a Jamaican accent."

Her answer only left Donovan waiting for another. He folded his arms across his broad chest. His size made him look like a giant against her dainty couch. "I'm confused."

British inhaled deeply, hating to explain her parents' oddities. "My dad was born and raised in Black Wolf Creek."

"Which you pointed out on the Ferris wheel the other night."

"Nice memory," British said with a nod.

"The company helped," Donovan replied with a wink.

"Anyway, my parents grew up just a few miles apart and it took a foreign exchange student photo shoot to bring them together. My mom was modeling at this big-time shoot and had just finished a semester overseas. The photographer needed an interpreter for another model and since my dad was friends with the photographer and right over at Clark Atlanta University, he came over to help."

"Was the model Jamaican?"

Confused, British shook her head. "No? Oh, because of the Jamaican accent my dad did? So, like I said, what attracted my mom to him was his way with foreign languages. The model who needed a translator was from Finland."

Donovan laughed. "Oh, okay, so what? They named your oldest brother after her country."

"I wish." British gulped and resisted the disgusted shiver creeping under her skin. "Let's just say we are all aware of each accent my dad used when they conceived us. For some people it's a song that puts them in a mood. For my mom it was my dad's accents."

It took him a moment to get what she meant. It took a minute and a half to stop laughing. "How did I miss this?"

"Trust me," she groaned, "I've gone through all types of attempts to forget it. As a kid it flew over my head, but as an adult, I understood and, for my sanity, I needed to leave the house."

Once Donovan sobered, he nodded. "I get it. I couldn't wait to move out when I turned eighteen."

"Did you live on your own?"

"For a few weeks I lived in the dorms and then I moved on to the frat house."

She rolled her eyes and headed into the kitchen. "Why am I not surprised?"

Donovan sat at the bar, which separated the kitchen and the living room. A set of four wineglasses hung from the rack, blocking his view. He tilted his head and winked.

"Don't believe the hype from the movies," he said. "It wasn't all parties and sorority girls."

British shook her head. "I didn't ask."

"We studied," Donovan went on.

"And partied," British added for him.

"Maybe a little, but you being all coupled up wouldn't have understood."

"Don't think I didn't party," British said. "Christian and I weren't always together throughout college. I played my fair share of beer pong. In private, of course."

"Didn't want word to get back to your boyfriend," he chuckled.

"No." She shook her head. "I didn't want to get caught by the pageant circuit's morality clause."

"What?" Donovan laughed even harder. "What kind of...?"

"I put a lot of time into becoming Miss Four Points," British said. "I lost the Miss Southwood crown to my best friend, Kenzie. But considering she and her family have a Miss Southwood dynasty, I still did pretty good for second place."

"Beauty queen dynasty? Moral clauses?" Donovan let out a sigh in jest.

"Don't act like the Ravens were free of scandal," British reminded him.

"You won't catch me in anything," he replied and picked up a lesson plan left on the counter. "I learned to keep my business to myself."

"Too bad social media didn't learn how to do the same for you."

Donovan clutched his heart. "Ouch."

British shrugged and teased him. "You can't help being so fast." She turned to the side-by-side fridge and opened it, trying to see what was in there. Anything left would be approaching at least a week old. "I have some frozen pizzas."

"Hey, I can't believe I'm saying this after all the food we ate yesterday and at lunch, but I could eat a horse."

British widened her eyes. "I thought by now you'd be careful with saying things like that."

Donovan nodded. "I stand corrected. I am hungry. We could take away or get delivery."

"Why do I get the feeling you don't want me cooking?"

"I enjoyed your cooking. The meal you made last week was fantastic. You just don't have to wait on me hand and foot. You've been out shopping with me just the same. And the reason we came over to your place was to crash since we're both tired and you didn't want me to drive."

"True," she agreed with a nod. "But I don't know if I can stay awake long enough for the food to get here. And you can't tell me you're not sleepy. You weaved in the road."

"It was your parents' driveway," Donovan explained, "and there was a football in the way."

Suddenly, British became nervous. It was one thing for a fling at a hotel where she wasn't going to have to stay much longer. But it was a whole different ball game in her own quarters. What choice did she have? It wasn't like she could let Donovan drive them down County Road 17 now. They were two mature adults.

They'd be able to stay the night together and be responsible. They'd managed to do so last night.

Donovan waved his hand toward the living room. "Come on, let's sit."

"Fine, let me grab the menus from this drawer." She fiddled with the utility drawer by her fridge and followed him into the other room. "Now we can figure out what we want to eat."

"I know what I want to eat," Donovan said with a coy smile.

Heat filled her cheeks, which she bit the inside of to keep from grinning. "You have a one-track mind."

"I think so when it comes to you." Donovan motioned for her to sit. She did at one end of the couch while he sat on the other. "What's going on with you?"

"Huh?" She gulped and looked over at him with her eyes, not moving her head.

Donovan adjusted himself into the corner of the couch. His left thigh was cocked on the cushions. "Are you nervous with me being here?"

"No," she lied. "Maybe a little."

"I can go back to the hotel, British. I meant it when I said I wanted to take things slow with you."

Yet she didn't want to take things slow. "This is just awkward with you being here and, no, I don't want you to leave. Deer season has picked up and with all the hunters out there searching for big game, I'd hate for a buck to run out on the road and cause you to swerve."

A passing car blared its horn in the street.

"Like what happened to Christian?"

A pinch of pain, a threat of tears rushed through British. "It's not fair to talk about that with you."

Donovan leaned across the couch and took her hand in his. "It is absolutely fair. We're together."

She cut her eyes at him and he nodded.

"I know it's crazy, British," he said softly. "I can't say what the future holds for us, but as of right now, I'm here with you. We're together. If you're in pain, I want to know why and what to do to solve it."

"I'm not in pain," she replied with a shaky voice. "I'm just. Afraid."

"Why?"

"I don't want to lose you." And then she realized eventually he would leave…and that was what she wanted, right? "I mean like that. In a tragic accident because of me."

"Christian's accident wasn't because of you, either," he said.

"What do you think we ought to eat?" British changed the subject and Donovan went along with it. They decided to order in Chinese food and watch some TV as they waited.

MET stayed true to its brand, airing several multicultural Christmas romance films. Halfway through the movie based on a Brenda Jackson book, their food arrived. Donovan straightened up her coffee table while she fixed a couple glasses of wine. They set their cartons of beef and broccoli, General Tso's chicken, spicy noodles, crispy honey wings, eggrolls, crab rangoon and Chinese doughnuts in front of them and sat with their legs crisscrossed on the floor. Donovan attempted to impress her with his use of chopsticks until he dropped a piece of broccoli on the table.

"I never would have pegged you as a romance fan," British teased him once the movie ended.

Donovan pulled himself up from the floor and sat with his back against his side of the couch. "It's Brenda Jackson," he said simply.

"One of your many girlfriends must have left her romance books behind," British mumbled and immediately regretted saying so. "Geez, I'm sorry. I must sound like a jealous girlfriend."

Donovan wiggled his brows at her. "Girlfriend."

It was hard to do anything but smile when around him. British instead rolled her eyes. She stood and gathered their empty containers.

"You can't believe everything you've read about me, British." Donovan stood to help, taking the containers into his hand.

"I didn't read it," she clarified. "I saw it all on social media."

"When did you look me up?"

"I did not." British pressed her hand against her heart. "But the girls did. And they showed me every single model you've dated in the last three years."

"Define 'dated.'"

"I don't have to define anything. I saw plenty of pictures."

"I can't help what's out there, British."

"No, but considering you gave Stephanie a pep talk about men learning how to respect women, you're a pig," she snarled and pushed past him. She was jealous. *Damn it.* "I only let them show me the PG-13 pictures. But don't get me started on the images that were highly inappropriate for girls to see on the internet without being eighteen."

Donovan held on to her elbow. "Wait a minute, now."

"You know what," she said with a sigh, "you really don't have to explain your past to me, Donovan."

"I do if your opinion of me drops." His voice softened and so did her stance. "You're the best thing that's happened to me in a while."

They did not need to have this conversation. This conversation led to promises and relationships. The most she could ask of him now was just for him to be himself.

"Donovannn," British drawled and pulled away from his firm hold.

"I work in the beauty industry, British," he said over her plea. British melted into his dark eyes. "You can't think I am sleeping with every single model I've been photographed with."

Silence built between them.

The television screen flickered to a commercial and a deep voice-over announced next Wednesday's installment.

"As you're finishing up the Thanksgiving weekend, don't forget to tune in to our inside look at Ravens Cosmetics as we break down the levels of the family."

Donovan let go of British's arm and searched through the empty containers and crab rangoon wrappers. "Not now, damn it," he groaned.

The voice-over continued. "We've followed the whirlwind romance between the CEO, Will Ravens, and his Creative Design Director, Zoe Baldwin. We've caught up with the twin sisters running public relations. Tomorrow night we'll take an inside look at their playboy brother. No, not Marcus Ravens, but the elusive Donovan Ravens, the one who only lets his picture be taken when he's with a mod—"

The screen went blank. Donovan breathed heavily in satisfaction with the remote control in his hand. "Television is overrated."

"Nice save." British laughed and turned back toward the kitchen. Donovan followed close behind. "I can do these dishes."

"I know you can, but I want to help."

"Fine." She blew out a sigh.

"But first, dessert."

Donovan dipped his head low and captured her mouth with his.

British forgot her thoughts. She only reacted. The moment his tongue touched hers, her eyes rolled to the back of her head. She tried not to moan but, like a starving woman, a growl escaped her throat. How was it possible to have missed his touch?

"Do you know how long I've been waiting to do that?" Donovan asked, breaking the kiss.

British wrapped her arms around his shoulders. "I have an idea."

The empty cartons dropped to the floor when Donovan scooped her up into his arms. "Where is your bedroom?"

She inclined her head and in no time they reached the closed door. "Wait, I need to prepare you for something," she said, holding on to the crystal doorknob.

With an easy smile, Donovan winked and covered the knob with his hand. "It's okay, British. I expect to see a photograph of you and Christian. It's natural."

"No, wait!"

Donovan crossed the threshold with her in his arms. He stopped walking any farther and craned his neck to take in the panoramic view of the posters. All one-hundred-plus photos of her New Edition collection over the years.

"In my defense—" she began to cringe, hiding her face in the crook of his shoulder "—when I moved here, I didn't want to start a new beginning with old photographs of me and Christian. So my high school friends and I got a little creative one day."

"A little drunk and creative?"

"Maybe just a little," British admitted. The morning after she and the Tiara Squad had finished decorating, British thought she'd gone back in time.

"Have you ever met them?" Donovan asked.

"No. I wouldn't want to embarrass myself." She lifted her head to find his eyes filled with amusement.

"The next time they're in town, I'm flying you in," he said before continuing their route to the bed.

The words played over in British's head. Not the exciting news about possibly meeting her all-time favorite boy band but the idea that Donovan was going to leave her. But this was what she'd wanted. Right?

Chapter 9

"You've got this," Stephanie said, closing her eyes and reaching for the hand beside her.

"We're all supporting each other," added Lacey.

Kathleen cleared her throat and nodded. "Ms. B told us we can do this. You can do this."

Touched by being mentioned in this pep talk slash motivational speech the Saturday morning after Thanksgiving, British placed her hand over her heart. Screams of excitement from the unexpected crowd rose from beyond the red curtain of the Christmas Wonderland scene created in the town center in Southwood. A line of eager children stretched down Main Street. The girls, dressed in red and green elf costumes, decided to pray for Donovan before he made his debut as this year's Southwood Santa.

"Let's bow our heads," Natasha nicely ordered everyone. "Dear Lord, we ask you to take time out of

Your busy schedule today and make today as successful as possible."

Everyone ended with a soft amen, except for one in the prayer circle.

"Amen," Donovan shouted and clapped his white-gloved hands together.

The white beard of the Santa suit he wore billowed with his breath. Despite the heaving padding against the eight-pack abs she'd caressed this morning, Donovan made playing Santa look sexy. Every visitor to sit on Santa's lap was allowed to do so if they donated a can or nonperishable item to help the Winter Harvest food bank. The event made sure everyone in Four Points had a holiday meal. British thought it was a great idea and even better with her STEM for GRITS team here now.

"I feel stupid," said Donovan.

Natasha squared off with Donovan, grabbing him by the shoulders. "You get out there and you be the best damn Santa Southwood has ever seen."

"'Tasha," British warned softly.

"Sorry," said Natasha. "You're going to be great."

The other girls, dressed in various combinations of elf outfits, rallied around the hot Santa and patted his red coat. The bells on the top of their pointy crescent-shaped hats jingled.

Donovan took a deep breath. "How did I get myself into this mess?" he asked British.

"You fell for my mother's charm," British explained.

Laughing, Donovan couldn't do anything but nod. "She can sell anything."

An emcee out front hyped the crowd a little more and brought in a roar of cheer and applause. British patted Donovan's back with her gloved hand. Like Donovan, she, too, had been manipulated by Joan, which explained why she stood behind the curtain ready to be called out to meet the waiting children.

To help sell the Winter Wonderland scene, British had recruited the girls to act as elves. Some of the fellows from the middle school's team built the set and created a spectacular snowy scene kids and adults would visit. The girls stepped out first and egged on the crowd, leaving Donovan and British alone for a brief moment. Their hands touched and even through the fabric, the heat rose.

"I really can't believe you're going through with this," British teased. She straightened the black rims of the glasses hanging low from Donovan's ears. He reached to wrap his arms around her waist but the padding prevented it.

"Damn this suit," he growled. "Can I get an IOU on the kiss?"

The emcee announced the arrival of Mrs. Claus. British patted Donovan's belly. "Let's see how you do with the kids today."

Before he could agree or not, British stepped out onto the stage for a warm welcome from the locals and visitors alike. She spotted her parents in the front with the grandkids and began to wave before realizing she didn't want to spoil the magic of Christmas for the little ones. The high school band played "Santa Claus Is Coming to Town" and at the drum solo, Donovan burst through the opening in the curtains. Everyone went wild.

The morning went by in a blur. Kids of all sizes came to sit on Santa's lap to tell him what they wanted. Stephanie walked the kids from the red, licorice-like path lined with giant red-and-white candy canes up to Santa's throne, where she handed British a card with the child's name so she could introduce Santa.

By noon she and Donovan were able to communicate well enough that she only needed to whisper the child's name to gain the element of surprise. Once the child said what he or she wanted, British wrote it down and gave it to Natasha, who handed it to the waiting parents on the other side of the line. A few cranky kids tugged at Santa's beard, exposing his face. The single mothers—and a few of the not-so-single mothers—all sighed at the sight of Donovan's dreamy smile.

The lunchtime crowd of kids was a bit stronger. A lot of them did not want to leave Santa's side without telling him exactly everything they wanted. Donovan let them sit a little longer, though Lacey did not mind huffing out her irritation. At least Donovan practiced patience when a few of the children gripped his biceps—which the lurking moms did not mind.

"Is it me," Stephanie asked, handing an elementary school–aged kid's card to British, "or are we starting to see the same children over and over?"

"I thought the same," said British. She looked at the card and mouthed the name to Donovan. She thought she knew everyone in town. Donovan, being the first African American Santa of the season, brought out the neighboring communities to the town center. Southwood's diverse community blended races, which made it possible to have a representative from every culture that celebrated Santa. Next weekend one of the Reyes brothers would don the suit.

"Hello, Gracie," Donovan greeted someone in his deep voice.

British headed back to where Stephanie stood. She peeked around at the never-ending line and smiled with satisfaction. She was proud at how focused the team members were…at least up until the moment another one of the GRITS girls from the after-school program ran over to whisper in Stephanie's ear.

"OMG," Stephanie gasped. "Excuse me, y'all," she said to the crowd and pushed her way through.

British shook her head and tried to remember these were adolescents. She picked up the slack and brought the next child over the red threshold. While she waited, British watched Donovan. For a man with such a playboy reputation, he certainly possessed a down-home quality. He was great with the children. He'd bonded with her nieces and nephews, all of whom she did not have to remind Donovan of their names. Part of British wondered what Donovan would be like as a dad. *Probably spoil the kids*, she thought.

"Be careful, dear," Joan teased, coming up behind British. "You look like you're falling for him."

"Whatever, Mother." British shrugged her mother's hug off and focused on Santa. Falling for him. Whatever. They bonded over hot sex and no promises. That worked for them, or at least that was the final compromise this morning before they'd left her bed.

"Excuse us," Stephanie bellowed, pulling a young girl by the hand to the front of the crowd. "Excuse us. VIP here."

"That's Quandriguez's sister," explained Kathleen. "She's deaf, you know."

"I know," said British.

The petrified young girl stood stock-still at the sight of Santa. She wore an ice-blue windbreaker with a blonde princess in a matching blue dress on the back.

Donovan motioned for her to step forward but not even his dazzling smile got her to budge. The crowd watched carefully. British rushed over to help but, like the girl, stood frozen. Donovan took off his glove and began to sign for the girl. At that moment the audience all gave a collective sigh and fell in love with this Santa a little more. Including British.

"Hey, Home Ec."

British cringed at the nickname and rolled her eyes at the moment being spoiled by none other than Cam Beasley. Given the Mrs. Claus outfit she'd had to wear, she decided to mind her manners. Besides, he was probably here with his kids. The last thing they needed was to be reminded of what a jerk they had for a father.

"Cam," British said with a droll eye-roll before turning around.

"I thought I recognized you," Cam said, coming up to the velvet rope. Two small children flanked him on either side. "I'm surprised to find you here."

Do not take the bait. Do not take the bait, she warned herself. "Well. I am." She smiled sweetly and adjusted the faux gold-framed glasses slipping down her nose.

"I figured you would be practicing."

"My girls are just fine," British said. She pulled the curls of the gray wig away from her face and bent to face the young boy and girl with him. "Are you guys excited to meet Santa?"

The sweet children nodded and cheered, ready for the introductions. British couldn't hold their father against them. She took their hands and led them up the walkway. Thankfully, Cam moved to the other side of the drop-off line to pick up his kids.

The next group of visitors stumped her. The gorgeous couple standing in the front didn't have a child with them. As a matter of fact, the next half dozen women didn't have children with them, just groups of girlfriends all pointing their cell phones at Santa.

"What is going on?" British asked Kathleen.

"The Southwood Santa is now viral and he's more like the sexy Santa."

British clutched the white fur collar around her throat. Her knees buckled. The back of her throat became dry. "Kathleen," she gasped, shocked at the photograph.

"What?" Kathleen shoved her bedazzled cell phone in British's face. "Everyone is talking about it."

Shielding the screen with her hand from the blaring afternoon sun, British looked at the photograph of the precise moment when a set of twins sat on Donovan's lap. One twin pulled down Donovan's beard while the other struggled to climb up his arm, thus pulling his red jacket open and exposing his buff chest and arms. Regardless of the twins' actions, Donovan stayed in character. Though she knew the story behind the photo, Donovan still won the prize for sexiest Santa. Her Sexy Santa, she thought. A jolt of excitement raced through her veins.

"Excuse me," a deep voice said behind her.

British turned and came face-to-face with the Greek letters across the shirt of a six-foot-plus man. She slowly looked up and cleared her throat. "You're going to have to stand behind the ropes, sir," she said boldly. "Does your child have a card?" Beyond his frame, she didn't see a kid near him. All day today unaccompanied children pushed themselves over the line, eager to see Santa.

"I am a child of God," said a familiar voice, stepping out from behind him. "That counts, right?"

"Zoe?" British shaded her eyes. "What on earth?"

Zoe Baldwin, now Ravens, pushed past the man British realized was her husband, Will Ravens, also known as Donovan's brother. She cast a glance over her shoulder to see if Donovan had noticed them. Cam's kids kept his attention.

"What are you doing in town?" British asked. "I thought you only returned for the summers."

The creative design director at Ravens Cosmetics had spent a few summers in Southwood. Her grandmother no longer ran the Mas Beauty School but the home still stood. It didn't surprise British to find Zoe back in town. Her father still lived here. As British hugged Zoe, she realized what a perfect match Zoe and Will made together. She was an expert makeup artist and Will was CEO of the world's best cosmetic company. It made sense for Zoe and Will to get together. It was as if destiny designed their future. Where did that leave British and Donovan?

"Girl, this outfit is everything," said Zoe, walking around British. While Zoe admired the Mrs. Claus look, British whistled at Zoe. Tall, thin, beautiful Zoe belonged on the cover of a magazine as well as in the pages. "I might need one for a little later." She elbowed Will in the ribs.

Will reached for Zoe's hand and managed to maneuver her in front of him and wrapped his hand around her waist. "By Christmas, you won't need any padding."

British's mouth dropped wide open. "Zoe, are you?"

Zoe pressed her finger to her mouth. "We're trying to find my folks to tell them before everyone else finds out."

"You know, I saw Miss Jamerica and my mom heading over to the Cupcakery." Joan and Zoe's mother, Jamerica Baldwin, modeled together back in the day.

"My mom is eating a carb?"

Back in the day, it was Joan who'd introduced Zoe's

parents to one another at one of their photo shoots held at Magnolia Palace.

"Stranger things have happened," said British. She turned her attention to Will, who let go of Zoe's belly with one hand and began filming Donovan with his cell phone. "Hey, now," she said to him. "You have to donate a canned good or money in order to get a picture with Santa or take pictures—that includes recording him."

Will narrowed his eyes on her. "Mrs. Claus?"

Perhaps it was because they were brothers, but British couldn't help but pick up on the arrogance of the man. She squared her shoulders. "I'm serious. The donations for today go to feed the hungry."

Will reached into his pocket and pulled out a wad of cash. "Will this do?"

British glanced back at Donovan. "Well, it's all in the name of charity—film your brother all you like."

The crowd around them began to disappear. The young elves, also known as the GRITS team, ran around with the other kids in the town square. To think a few nights ago this center had been transformed into a fall festival and was now a winter carnival. A safe, bright and loud merry-go-round spun on one corner of the square. The line there matched the line for Santa. The smell of funnel cakes, grilled hot dogs and popcorn floated through the crisp air. All Donovan wanted to do was to grab something to eat and head back to British's place, since it was closer than Magnolia Palace.

By the end of his shift as the Southwood Santa, Donovan sat back on his red-velvet throne. He kind of wished more parents would bring their children just so he could avoid speaking with Will, who'd clearly enjoyed exploiting Donovan's job today. Why didn't it click in his head, when Will told him he and Zoe were going off for the holidays, that they'd come here to Southwood? Every half hour for the rest of the afternoon Will had stood down by the photographer and annoyingly filmed him. The camera caught every bad moment such as when a kid almost lost his lunch on Donovan, a diaper leak and a few candy canes stuck in his fake beard. The one redeeming part of the afternoon was the connection he shared with British. They were so in sync. The pit of his stomach flopped when she approached him.

"Hey," British said, coming close. The sweet scent of her intoxicating perfume flooded him. His stomach growled. "Are you hungry?"

"For food?" Donovan teased, wiggling his brows.

"Careful, Santa," she said playfully. "I overheard your brother Will talking about taking you for dinner at Valencia's. It's another spot you have to try before you leave."

The top portion of Donovan's lip curled. One, partly because his brother being in town threatened to take away time from British and, two, the idea of leaving loomed in the back of his head.

"Give me five minutes to get rid of him." He gave a sinister laugh and rubbed his hands together.

Donovan took a step forward but British placed her hand on his forearm. "You can't kill him right now."

"Because I'm dressed as Santa?" If that were the case, Donovan was ready to get out of the red costume now. British and Donovan waved once more to the onlookers and posed for a few more pictures as Mr. and Mrs. Claus. They received a round of applause before a few of the elves opened the curtain for them to exit.

Just before they disappeared, British shook her head

back and forth, grinning and speaking through her teeth, "Because we're going to have a civilized dinner."

"And then I can kill him?"

"No." She linked her hand in his but not before slipping off her white glove and his.

The skin-to-skin contact was so needed since he wasn't able to kiss her right now. Given the only privacy they had was a strung-up sheet, Donovan decided acting on impulse—to take British into his arms right now—needed to wait. After eight hours of playing Santa and being on his p's and q's, he needed some one-on-one time with British. For Donovan the suit jacket with the three giant black-plastic buttons on the front came off easily. Knowing it was going to be hot underneath, he hadn't bothered putting on a shirt.

The Mrs. Claus dress required help, which Donovan didn't mind. Again, the two moved in unison and without words. British took off her hat and gray wig, then lifted her dark curls off her neck and exposed her back to him. Donovan resisted raising her skirts and showing her just how much he wanted her right now. An excited scream from a girl outside the area stopped him. Regretfully, Donovan rebuttoned British's costume. Kissing her neck, he swatted her bottom.

"Did you have fun today?" British asked him, turning around in his arms.

"I hate to admit it, but I did." Donovan never thought he'd have a blast playing a married man. They walked down the red carpet toward Will and Zoe. Zoe he liked. Will? Donovan balled his fists together. But as they approached his little brother, Donovan's irritation settled and he reached out to hug him.

"What the hell are you doing here, man?" Will asked

him, patting him on the back. "Have you been here this whole time?"

"Yep," Donovan answered.

Despite the latest pressures of the job making the youngest member of the Ravens family act like a tyrant lately, Donovan knew he couldn't stay mad at Will. Will had never asked to be the CEO of the company and Donovan had played his part by nominating him to be at the helm. Will had just come off a career-ending soccer injury, and Donovan had known he'd needed something else to focus on. And he'd been right. Will's vision for bringing classic beauty back to the company had helped refresh the sales. Donovan had seen the financial reports.

"You're such a copycat," Will joked. "This is my hideaway spot."

Zoe stepped between the two men to give Donovan a hug. "Don't be mad at Donovan for having good taste. Hey, brother-in-law."

"Hey, sister-in-law," Donovan replied. "You look as beautiful as ever."

"Thank you."

"So beautiful, I think you should grace the face of Ravens." Donovan gave Will as smirk before letting Zoe go.

"You're not getting off that easy," Will said, tugging his wife's elbow so she fit in the crook of his shoulder when he draped his arm over her shoulders. "You still need—"

Zoe silenced him with a squeeze to the hand. "Sweetie, we're on vacation."

"Speaking of which…" Will began. "Where did you spend Thanksgiving?"

"Here," Donovan said.

"With my family." British spoke up. "Hi, we haven't officially met."

"Oh my God," Zoe knocked herself in the head with the palm of her hand. "Where is my brain?"

Zoe, Will and British laughed at some inside joke, which baffled him. Donovan cleared his throat to break up the camaraderie. "Will, allow me to introduce you to someone very special, British Carres. British, this is my annoying little brother, Will, and his—"

"British and I go way back," said Zoe, with the flick of her left wrist, waving the Ravens family heirloom engagement ring When Will had asked for it from their grandmother, Donovan couldn't have been more pleased. He loved Zoe but wondered if it would be rude to ask for it back when the time was right. Donovan gulped at the thought. Prior to coming to Southwood Donovan was sure he'd never get married. And now here he was, not sure if he wanted to leave without taking British as his wife. The notion was a pleasant surprise. British made him happy.

Will extended his hand to British. "Pleased to meet you. Thanks for allowing me to film Donovan."

Donovan looked between the two of them. "What's that?"

"Well…" British began, her cheeks turning his favorite reddish hue. "This is for charity and with the load of cash your brother dropped, we're able to feed everyone in Four Points whether they need it or not."

"My humiliation for charity, huh?" Donovan accepted with a nod. "I suppose no one is going to recognize me."

Again the three of them shared a laugh.

"Oh, honey," British cooed, "I don't know how to tell you this but you're Southwood famous now."

Whatever that meant, Donovan didn't care, just as long as it got British to move against his frame. As natural as it felt, he wrapped his arm around her shoulders and pretended to ignore Will's questioning gaze at the intimate touch.

"Is that Maggie Swayne?" Zoe asked, shielding her eyes from the setting sun. "She's been MIA in Miami for a while now."

"Speaking of missing…" Will said. "Donovan, what's going on with your search for the next spokesmodel?"

Now was not the time to discuss work. Donovan heaved a heavy sigh and tugged British closer to him. "I had a great idea. Didn't I?"

"Not on your life, buddy," said British.

Zoe squealed and clapped her hands. "That would be so perfect. British, with your pageant background, you'd be perfect."

"I am a professional *STEM* teacher," British declared.

"I majored in chemistry—" Zoe shrugged "—and it's time to show the world that girls can dominate the science lab and the runway at the same time."

For a breath of a second, British bit her bottom lip, giving Donovan a sliver of hope that Zoe's motivational point of view might work. "As I told Donovan before, I can't very well sell makeup to impressionable girls."

Will snorted as if offended.

A protective surge electrocuted Donovan's veins. "She is an awesome teacher," he said. "She could teach you a thing or two."

"Can she teach me how to find the perfect cover girl?" Will asked and shrugged. "You know what? I'll just go with the original plan and hire—"

Thankfully a group of teenagers playing tag ran past

them, shutting Will up before Donovan did so with his fist. He didn't want Tracy's name mentioned and ruining this great day. Parents moved from store to store with packages in their hands. Children ran around unsupervised. What a difference between raising kids in a metropolis city and a small town like this one. Or living in a warm environment like the Woodburys' home.

An elementary-aged child skipped by, licking the chocolate frosting right off the top of a cupcake. The dollop fell to the ground and his tears began to flow. While Donovan looked around for the boy's mother, British knelt to soothe him. "Let's get you another one," British said and looked up at Zoe. "Want to come with me? We can go say hi to Maggie."

"And get this kiddo another scoop of frosting for his cupcake, huh?" Zoe bent over and tweaked the little boy's nose.

British reached for Zoe's hand, stopping to flutter her lashes at Donovan. His heart swelled and slammed against his chest at the thought of him having to leave eventually; the last thing he wanted was to be separated from her.

"So they're just going to walk off with someone's kid?" Will asked and shook his head. "We should call the police and let them handle it."

"British is a well-known teacher here in Southwood," Donovan explained. "She grew up here and I am willing to bet anything she knows the kid's parents." Just then, Mrs. Fitzhugh walked by and waved, calling Donovan out by name. "Everyone knows everyone around here."

With a side eye glance, Will hummed. "Mmm-hmm. Well, I'll never get used to that in Miami. Maybe in our grandparents' neighborhood."

"Speaking of," Donovan said. "How was Thursday with Grandma Naomi?"

"Traditional as usual," Will replied. "Catered dinner served at exactly one and a football game between us and the anti-cousins."

The anti-cousins were the group of relatives who'd tried to break the company up and start their retirements forty years early. Donovan was pretty sure it must have been an awkward holiday meal.

"We worked out our aggression during the game," Will said with a gloating laugh.

While the Woodburys played football, too, with just one casualty, Tom, Donovan could only imagine the carnage on the Ravens property. What he liked about the Woodburys was being able to play a good game and having fun.

A cool breeze blew but the new fond memories of British and her family kept him warm.

"Wow," Will gasped, breaking Donovan out of his trance as he watched British walk away. "You got it bad."

Without turning his head, Donovan cut his eyes at his brother. He reached out and grabbed Will by the shoulder, squeezing his clavicle. "Yes."

Chapter 10

The end of the Thanksgiving season kicked off the winter celebrations, as well as brought back Ramon and Kenzie Torres from their vacation at his family home. British thanked her friends for opening up Magnolia Palace to everyone with a basket of muffins and gossip. Kenzie was ecstatic to learn about a potential relationship between British and Donovan, knowing her matchmaking scheme had worked out for the better. The end of the fall season also brought British back to some rushed normalcy in her life. The GRITS girls were able to move back into their homes. The school doors opened up again and British went back to her life. The only difference this time was that Donovan still lingered…and she didn't mind. Even though she felt empty without him around as much, she had to get back to her regularly scheduled life.

Southwood also kicked off the start of the Christmas

holiday by decorating the town tree. There were a few more weeks until school let out for the three-week winter break and a lot more lessons to get through in the classroom. To top it all off, tonight was the big STEM competition for the Christmas Advisory Council. All the girls' hard work over the last two weeks was about to pay off.

For Donovan, the last two days had been busy working with Will to find the next face for Ravens Cosmetics. British knew she'd be lying if she said she didn't feel a twinge of jealousy at sending Donovan over to Grits and Glam Gowns.

Lexi Pendergrass Reyes owned not just the premier dress boutique in town but also a talent studio around the corner. British found herself coming over to the shop during her lunch break for one excuse or another. It's why she had the 3D Advent calendar on the corner of her desk now, plus a party dress for the school dance next week. Her pop-up visits hadn't soothed her insecurities.

Gorgeous women from every direction of Georgia came through the shop for advice and dresses. And she'd sent the perpetual bachelor into the lion's den. While British molded the minds of tomorrow's youth, Donovan held interviews that would change the life of one local lady. Somehow, British dreaded the day Donovan would come home and tell her he'd found the new face of RC. When he found the future face, there'd be nothing keeping Donovan in Southwood.

Initially, British had wanted a temporary situation— a playboy like Donovan, with a healthy fear of commitment. Sure, he'd had a reputation of being a ladies' man, but since they'd been together British had never seen that side of him. He was attentive, romantic and sweet.

Her family adored him and Donovan seemed to enjoy spending time with them. All of this happiness was going to end eventually when he found his perfect girl.

At the idea of being closer to Donovan, British actually considered taking him up on his daily offer to be the new face of Ravens Cosmetics. But her life was here in Southwood, at Southwood Middle School.

Another thing British usually hated to hear was the cruel sound of the afternoon bell ringing. It signaled the end of the day and reminded her that she'd run out of time to go over her well-thought-out lesson plans with her students. British waited for her students to leave the classroom before she headed over to city hall. The STEM teams were excused for the day for the competition. British hoped the girls were off to a good start. She expected a win, which would then take up her afternoons for a while to prepare for the District STEM Competition. With the girls participating in the STEM-Off now, British's afternoon was free. She planned to hang out at school until the final activity bell rang.

"So I hear our middle school kids are dominating the competition."

British tried not to shudder at the sound of Cam's voice. When she looked up from her attendance book, she found the director standing at the doorway, his arms crossed over his chest. A long dreadlock fell over his shoulder. In another lifetime she guessed he could have been considered handsome, but his attitude was atrocious. British pushed away from her desk. She buttoned the middle of her white lab coat and squared her shoulders. "Are you here to try to psych me out?" British asked him, rolling her yellow pencil between her fingers.

"I was actually coming to see if you wanted to up the ante."

"Meaning?"

"I mean there's not enough room for the both of us here, Home Ec."

A crack came from her hand where she'd snapped the pencil. "I've asked you before to stop calling me that."

"Why?" Cam placed his hands on his hips. The hem of the blue-plaid shirt he wore flopped over the waistband of his brown corduroy pants. "Let's be honest here."

She widened her eyes. "You mean you've been holding back on me?" British feigned a gasp. "What do you want?"

"I want the lab to myself from here on out."

"You're the director of the science department, Cam, not the owner of it," she clarified.

"I'm talking about when my boys win. I want you to resign."

British laughed; she bent over and laughed so hard that tears formed in her eyes. "You can't be serious," she asked once she sobered and placed her hands on her hips in the same stance as the director. "I'm surprised you didn't challenge me to a duel."

"Right about now, I'd take it," said Cam. He advanced into the room and let the heavy black door slam behind him.

For a moment British wasn't sure if she needed to be afraid. Lucky for her she had two older brothers who'd taught her how to protect herself. British stepped back in her black heels, in preparation to do battle. She even put her hands up. "Back up, Cam."

"It is Dr. Beasley," Cam said in a clipped tone. "And what is this? A little girl like yourself is going to try to beat me up?" He stepped closer.

A moment ago British wasn't sure of his intentions

but now Cam made it perfectly clear. His fists were balled at his sides. "I am so tired of watching you tip-toe around these halls acting like you own the place."

"I don't do that," said British, "but I am warning you to back away from me, Cam."

"I'm the boss here. It's best you remember—"

Since he kept advancing toward her, British extended her right fist and popped him in the nose. The punch didn't do anything but anger him more.

"Jesus, woman, you are reckless."

"And you're still getting in my face."

Cam didn't stop. He stepped even closer. The scent of the cafeteria lunch of chicken parm and garlic bread loitered on his breath. "I need you to leave the school, British."

"Cam." British curled her fingers around his to break the grip he'd taken on the lapels of her coat. "I am warning you."

"Are you going to leave when you lose?"

"Absolutely not," she replied. Her heart slammed against her chest. The band practiced right outside her window; she wasn't sure if the blaring trumpets would cover her screams. School was over and her girls were off getting ready for the STEM-Off this evening. "And when I win, I want you to stay here and watch my girls take over the lab four days out of the week. Now, if you know what's good for you, you'll let me go."

Cam sneered so hard she saw a piece of parsley wedged between his left bicuspid. "What are you going to do, hit me again?"

"No," boomed a deep voice. A beefy brown hand clamped down on Cam's shirt collar and pulled him back from her. "I am."

British's heart swelled at the sight of Donovan coming to the rescue.

Donovan jerked Cam's hands behind his back and slammed his head down on British's desk.

"Now, before you begin to cry out from the pain," Donovan said, "you're going to apologize for your behavior."

The way Donovan's hand pressed against Cam's cheek, there was no way for the man to speak. His dreads flopped in his face while a thousand veins popped in his forehead.

British folded her arms across her chest, pissed off. This man, who'd attempted to threaten her, had the nerve to look so pitiful right now.

"I can't hear you," Donovan growled. The silver cuff links on his suit jacket pressed into Cam's face.

"Don't kill him," British said.

"Who is this guy?"

"This is the director of the science department. The girls are going up against his boys in a couple of hours."

Donovan stepped back and let Cam up but not before spinning him around and grabbing him the same way Cam had grabbed British a few minutes ago. Donovan lifted Cam off his feet and brought his face near. "I'm only letting you live so you can see those girls beat your team. After that I never want to hear about you coming near my lady again. Do I make myself clear?"

My lady?

Had this been a cartoon scenario, the path Cam took to run out of the classroom would have been on fire right now. Donovan crossed his arms over his chest, looking satisfied with himself, and turned to face her. Then his eyes roamed hers. There wasn't a lot of distance between them but Donovan closed it immediately. "Are you okay?"

"I'm fine," she said, pushing his hands away as they roamed over her body.

"He didn't try to…"

When she realized what he implied, British shook her head. She pulled a stray curl behind her ear. "Good God, no. He was just trying to scare me." She left out the part that he'd done a good job.

"I don't think he's going to try anything like that again."

"Well I should say not," British scoffed. "Thanks to man-save-woman." To reiterate she grunted like a caveman.

Still dressed in the dark suit he wore to interview hot girls today, Donovan loosened the red paisley tie around his neck. "Are you calling me a caveman?"

"*Neanderthal* is the more correct term." She practically spouted the fact.

"Are you seriously going to be politically correct with me about what to call a caveman?" Donovan pressed his lips together to keep from laughing. "Come here, woman."

Though Donovan tugged at the middle button of her lab coat, British gave a little bit of resistance. "I can't believe you barged in here like that."

"What do you mean?" Donovan paid her pout no mind and nuzzled his chin against the crook of her neck. "You mean when I walked in here as you were getting mauled by some jerk?" He nibbled her jugular and her eyes fluttered. "I apologize if I got a little crazy. But I didn't appreciate the woman I love being assaulted."

Knees weak, British pushed against Donovan's chest. "Wait. What?"

"Love, British." Donovan tipped British by the chin with his thumb, getting her to see the seriousness in his eyes. Her breath fluttered. "I've never said it and meant it, British. I love you."

Love. The word seemed so simple. Is that what she had been feeling? "Donovan."

The final afternoon bell rang. Donovan dipped his head and kissed her lips, wiping any frayed nerves left over from her altercation with Cam. He pulled his mouth away. Eyes lingered on hers. "I don't need to hear you say it back. Not yet. Let's go watch the girls win."

"And why are we here?" Will leaned over and asked Donovan in the auditorium of city hall.

"Shh," Zoe whispered over her shoulder from where she sat in front of them to pay attention to the competition on the stage.

Not everyone in town filled the seats as Donovan had expected. It shocked him to find the disappointment rising in him over the lack of support the science teams received. He guessed most of the cheering crowds were parents of the participants. In his seat in the risers, Donovan couldn't have been prouder, not just for the girls but also for himself. He'd finally said the words he felt. He loved British. With Tracy, they'd dated six weeks and he still wasn't sure. With British, Donovan just knew. Every feeling—happiness, joy—felt right.

As of right now, the last two teams standing were the STEM for GRITS and the boys' robotics team from Southwood. British sat in the row behind the judges. From Donovan's understanding, when the girls advanced through each round, they were allowed to bring a member of their team, expanding from the original four: Stephanie, Lacey, Natasha and Kathleen. There were now two extra girls helping them.

The girls had taken Donovan's suggestion and come up with a few holiday-themed suggestions. His favorite had been the one from Stephanie. She'd created a mood necklace with quartz glass and thermotropic liquid crystals to demonstrate the various heat levels. In the beginning of the experiment, the girls passed out crystals to the mothers in the audience. They also selected few random boys in the audience on the robotics team—including the Quandriguez fellow Stephanie had a crush on. The goal at the end of the demonstration for each participant was to keep the mood rock at a teal color, which meant a calm state, and the orders were to make sure the mothers remained teal during the holidays.

For a bonus round the GRITS team paraded in front of the boys' team wearing various mood rocks. The girls brought the mothers of the committee onstage, handed them noise canceling earphones and then one by one listed off all the shopping, errands, decoration duties, holiday parties and everything needed for a smooth Christmas to each mother. To some, the girls said that everything was fine. The mood rocks for the mothers with less to do turned teal. The rings for the other mothers turned black, meaning they were stressed. The suggestion for the children of the mothers onstage was for them to know when to pitch in and help their moms or stay out of the way.

As for the boys, the girls examined their rocks, all while still wearing their various forms of jeans, T-shirts and turtlenecks. By the end of the experiment all the boys' mood rocks stayed in the red zone, which varied between excited and stimulated. For Cam's sake, the girls changed their variable each time by changing outfits, and no matter what they wore, from a lab coat to a pair of shorts and T-shirt or even a turtleneck, the boys were still distracted. The demonstration received a standing ovation from the mothers, female teachers and Donovan, as well.

Cam sneered and sank lower in his seat. Donovan's palms itched to be wrapped around his throat.

"See that girl," Donovan said, pointing at Stephanie, who was front and center wearing a pink-Bedazzlered lab coat. "She's going to be a future Ravens Cosmetics employee."

"She's a bit young to be the company's face," said Will. "I was looking for someone older. Speaking of which, can we end this search, get out of Southwood and just hire Tracy? She's been all over social media, which works in our favor."

Zoe twisted in her seat. "Excuse me?"

"I love Southwood, babe." Will corrected himself and leaned over to kiss his wife on the cheek.

"Don't forget my dad wants to sell the house," she said, "and we could easily move back here."

Donovan's laugh froze and an idea popped into his head. The Mas house had once been used as a classroom and family home. Zoe's great-grandmother had taught young ladies the chemistry behind makeup as well as how to sell beauty products and styling. Many of her students had worked with Donovan's grandparents, who'd run the place in the early days of Ravens Cosmetics. Considering Miami was the home base for RC, having a satellite office might be ideal. He crunched the numbers in his head and in his heart.

He'd meant it when he said he loved British. He would do anything to stay with her.

"Look," Will continued once his wife stopped giving him the evil eye. "Like the rest of us featured on Dana's bright idea of a reality show, Tracy got hold of the prereleased episode airing tonight."

There'd been a large attachment from MET Studios in Donovan's work email earlier this week. He'd ignored it and focused on the thousands of corporate emails delegated to his job. During what time he did have to spend with British, television was the last thing on his mind.

"She wasn't even in anything," Donovan said bitterly. "When I left, I didn't say a word to her. I didn't wake her up or anything."

Will leaned forward with his elbows on his knees and his fingers pressed to his temple. "What?"

"I was never on film with her. Why would she be included?"

"Donovan, she's been tweeting for the last twenty-four hours about a huge secret."

The pit of his stomach dropped. "What secret?"

"The hell if I know," Will said, shaking his head.

Donovan reached into the lining of his suit jacket and extracted his cell phone. Nothing happened. He couldn't get a signal. "I need to reach Amelia Reyes," he said.

"Amelia?" Zoe turned around again in her seat. "She was actually in town. You know she's from here."

Now that he thought about it, Amelia was the one who'd recommended Donovan come here to hang out after they filmed. "I don't have her number."

"C'mon." Zoe pushed away from her seat awkwardly and handed Will her program. "We'll be right back."

Will chuckled and rolled his eyes. "I'm coming, too."

Donovan hated to skip out on the crowning portion of the competition but he knew the girls were going to win. They had it in the bag, thanks to Kathleen's coding of a train robot with a vacuum that went around the stem of a Christmas tree and cleaned up pine needles and broken ornaments while it played Christmas songs.

Together, the threesome headed up toward the exit and down the hallway of city hall. Zoe was already whipping out her phone and dialing by the time they reached the glass entrance. A bright light blinded them the moment they stepped outside. Donovan angled his head to see better. A few dozen white vans were positioned at the front of the building with twice as many reporters standing in front of them, microphones, booms and recorders facing them.

An anger bubbled inside Donovan. Why couldn't these reporters show up for the competition at the beginning and stay? There was plenty of room for everyone...maybe not their equipment, but still. Imagine the confidence it would have given the students to see their hard work be recognized not just by their colleagues but by the outside world. Donovan understood British's passion for the kids.

"It's going straight to voice mail..." said Zoe. Her words trailed off at the sight of everyone standing in front of them.

Donovan hated the spotlight. He sensed the heat of the lamp on his scar and felt it amplified by the world. He turned around to leave.

"Mr. Ravens," someone called out.

Naturally, Will stepped forward. He was the head of RC and knew what to say in front of an audience. "Good evening, ladies and gentlemen," he said with a surefire cocky chuckle. "Are you here to get the Black Friday scoop on our items?"

Coming to his aid, Zoe appeared by Will's side. "Of course not, sweetheart," she said to him. "I'm sure everyone's gotten wind of the exciting things brewing inside city hall." She smiled like the dazzling director of creative design that she was. "You guys, come on and see the brilliant young minds of our future leaders."

Good job, Donovan thought. The girls needed the spotlight, especially if they were to walk outside any moment now with their trophy in hand. As much as he wanted to see them win, he needed to get to the bottom of this surprise Tracy might have. He scrolled through his phone to find the emails he'd never looked at. Cell service in the building was poor. The attachment was large and kept pausing, probably due to the satellite of the news crews.

"We're here for the Sexy Santa," someone yelled.

Will turned to glance at Donovan, who was completely confused until he remembered the photographs taken at the winter carnival last weekend. A few shots were still floating around town. He thought it was local. The Southwood Santa, he believed, was what the waitress called him at the coffee shop across the street from the gown shop.

"Excuse us for a moment," Will said. He motioned for Donovan and Zoe to huddle together at the doors of the entrance to city hall. Beyond the glass, they spotted a crowd coming toward them. "Let's take this opportunity to market our new men's line. We have those lotions and colognes coming out for Christmas."

"No," Donovan declared. He craned his neck to find British's curly head coming their way.

"Are you listening to me?" Will asked.

"Not really," he huffed in response.

"Dana and Eva are our PR people," said Zoe. "They'd agree that any publicity is good publicity, Donovan. They know you as the Sexy Santa. You could promote the perfect stocking stuffer for people."

"Hell no." Donovan wasn't sure how many ways he

needed to make himself clear to them. "I am not taking this opportunity to put the shine on British and her team to sell products for Ravens."

"Think about the girl you pointed out," Will pleaded. "Stephanie, the one you said was going to be a future employee of ours. Talk about the chemistry put into our products."

"Definitely," Zoe said excitedly.

In the reflection of the bright lights of the cameras behind them, a glare glazed the glass doors. Donovan couldn't see inside but he did see Amelia Reyes shouldering her way through the crowd with the help of the guy who worked at the real-estate office next door to the dress shop where they'd held interviews this week. *Nate Reyes, that was it*, Donovan thought. Nate had a few other people behind him.

"Amelia."

"Donovan," Amelia breathed heavily, holding her cell phone in the air. "The tracker works."

What the hell was going on?

"What tracker?" Zoe and Will chorused.

The crowd behind them grew louder. Nate and his group made a blockade of sorts for privacy. Now Donovan felt trapped. He wanted to see British.

"There's a Sexy Santa Tracker website," Amelia explained. She showed her phone to them and, sure enough, on the screen, there was a cartoon figure of Amelia standing next to one of the photos from the winter carnival in front of city hall.

Will reached for the phone for a better view. "This is creepy."

"Stalkerish," Zoe added.

An incoming call blurred the photo. Donovan caught Christopher Kelly's name flash across the screen. Why was the president of MET calling Amelia after nine in the evening? Tonight's reality show. What the hell happened on the show?

"Donovan, you have to believe me," said Amelia, "I approved one version of your segment."

This did not sound good. He waited for Amelia to explain what happened but the reporters and now ever-growing crowd of onlookers had started oohing and aahing too loudly to hear her answer. Suddenly, Tracy appeared, decked out in a red, skintight, damn-near-see-through catsuit, and sauntered up the steps. She wore a pair of oversize black glasses and a white scarf over her head, which she pulled down to let the material fall across her shoulders, making her look like an adult-star version of Mrs. Claus.

Oh damn, Donovan thought. She needed to go. Donovan moved through the surrounding crowd to reach her.

Tracy slipped her glasses off with her left hand. The vaguely familiar gaudy ring Donovan had spotted the morning he'd returned to his condo glittered under the lights.

"We can't fix this, Mr. Kelly," Amelia was screaming into the phone. "She's already here."

"Tracy!"

"Tracy!"

Reporters shouted her name. The highly sought-after model spun slowly on her spiked patent-leather boots and faced the crowd.

"You're dressed like a mighty damn sexy Mrs. Claus," someone pointed out.

"You see—" Tracy started to speak but Zoe reached for Tracy's elbow and jerked her backward.

To not stumble or fall, Tracy offered an apologetic smile to the audience and reluctantly went off with Zoe before Donovan grabbed her. Will opened the door for them to enter and the waiting crowd outside began to pour onto the front steps. People oblivious to the happenings outside found themselves pushing their way forward past defeated children, some with tears on their faces. Tracy snaked her hand out and grabbed hold of Donovan's. Will, Zoe, Tracy and Donovan made a human train inside the foyer of city hall.

"Are you nuts?" Tracy yelled at Zoe and snatched her arm away, as did Donovan. Her high-pitched voice echoed against the marble walls.

"What did you think you were about to announce?" Zoe asked.

Ever the actress, Tracy reached for Donovan again. This time he screwed his face up and shook his head.

"Tell me you haven't missed me," Tracy demanded.

"Not in the slightest," Donovan laughed.

"Then why did you give me this?" Tracy held her hand in the air. "I found it in the drawer when you gave me a few minutes to collect my belongings."

Zoe gasped. "Donovan, you didn't."

"Of course I didn't," Donovan snapped.

Amelia made her way into the foyer. "He didn't give you that ring, Tracy," she said. "My associate thought it would be a great storyline for the Ravens family. I just found out he planted the ring in the drawer."

Blinking in disbelief, Tracy shook her head. "I don't understand. I gave you the best six weeks of my life."

Donovan squinted his right eye. "Me and that guy you brought into my house and my bed."

At least Tracy had the decency to shut her mouth. "We can work past that, Donovan." She attempted to reach for him but he recoiled. Tracy's red lips curled into a sneer. "Jesus. I've tolerated looking at you for months and now you want to treat me like this. My God, don't act like you didn't tell me you loved me."

Amused, Donovan scratched his faced, his fingertips touching his beard. He shrugged his shoulders. "You can't hold me accountable for what was said in bed. Let's call it momentary insanity," he said, inclining his head.

"Donovan," Will warned.

Tracy was the epitome of why Donovan had remained a bachelor for so long. He shook his head and chuckled, thinking of the woman he had now. He needed to see British. So when Tracy stormed out of the way, he took a deep breath to leave but it was too late. Tracy's height masked British behind her.

As to how long British had stood behind Tracy, he had no idea. But judging by the look of horror on her face—as well as the GRITS team who stood behind British holding their trophy—she'd been there long enough.

"British…"

Zoe and Amelia ushered the girls out the front door. Will waited behind.

The corners of British's lips turned down. Her cheeks turned a darker hue than the one he'd grown accustomed to love.

"Seven hours ago you told me you loved me," she said in a hoarse whisper.

"Love," Donovan corrected. His heart ached seeing her upset. "I love you, British."

"That's just something you say," British said, stepping back, away from his touch. "Like you told her."

"But I didn't mean it." Donovan tried to reach for British's hand but she folded her arms across her chest. His heart ached at her rejection. All eyes turned to him.

British's mouth dropped. "Wow."

"C'mon, British, you know it's not like that. Yes, I was in a relationship with Tracy. You were aware of that. Before you, I've never felt love before. I've never been in love with anyone like I am with you. I need you, British. Tell me you need me. Tell me you're mad, but don't walk away from us. You have to believe me. Surely you know how I feel about you."

"What I do know—" British pointed at him "—is that you're exactly what I thought you were when we first met. A free-loving playboy floating from woman to woman to bide your time until the next one. What was I, your Southwood flavor of the month until you left to go back to Miami?"

"I've changed, British, and you know it." Donovan's arms flopped to sides. "You have to stop comparing me to your Christian. I'm not perfect but I will always love you."

"Oh," she scoffed, "there's no comparison. Christian may have suffered from an enlarged heart, but you, Donovan Ravens, don't have one at all."

"Ms. B," Stephanie said, poking her head around the corner of the hallway. "My parents had to go back to Magnolia Palace and wondered if you could bring me back."

Just like that, British inhaled deeply and tore her eyes away from Donovan. The cold glare chilled him to the bone. He reached for her fingertips, which, for a brief second, she allowed him to touch. She paused by his shoulder. Donovan leaned down to kiss the top of her head. "Don't do this, British."

"I can't be a good role model of a strong woman and believe the words you so frivolously give out. Goodbye, Donovan."

Chapter 11

"I feel like every time I meddle with a Ravens's love life I seem to make things worse," said Kenzie.

British hugged her body and leaned against the door of her car. She'd just dropped off Stephanie with her parents and wasn't in the mood for heading home just yet, knowing Donovan would be waiting at her place to talk further. There was nothing left to say. He admitted to saying things that weren't true, like that he loved Tracy. How was she supposed to believe him now? On top of that, his callous behavior toward that woman, Tracy, was in poor taste, especially in front of her students.

By the time she'd reached Magnolia Palace, the exposé or documentary on Donovan's portion of the Ravens story had already aired. On top of everyone in Southwood seeing it, Tracy wore a ring she said Donovan gave her. Everyone in British's family left messages for her to call. Everyone wanted to know how she was doing or what was going on. Enough people at city hall had overheard the quarrel between Tracy and Donovan, and then with her. Small towns and gossip…

She sniffed. "This isn't your fault, Kenzie," she said to her friend. "I initiated things with Donovan knowing full and well he was a perpetual bachelor playboy who would leave. This is what I get for being so fast." She tried to laugh through the pain. It hurt to know she'd foolishly opened her heart to someone who only walked away, making her feel like a fool. The night was not supposed to end like this. Tonight she was going to celebrate the girls winning and tell Donovan she loved him, too. And she did. Or she thought she did. British was confused.

"You weren't being fast. You were testing the waters. Had you married that first yahoo from Peachville, I would say that was fast."

First Vonna knew about British's failed dating life and now Kenzie. "How did you know?"

"I've been Southwood's historian for a while now," Kenzie said, reaching over and pushing British's shoulders. "I tracked down a story for the gala last summer and saw you leaving a restaurant with some man."

A cold breeze whipped through the air. Again British smelled the faint burning of wood, like she had the first time she'd met Donovan. This time of year she figured a group of hunters had set up camp somewhere nearby. She considered taking post at a deer stand just to avoid everyone.

"Anyway, I feel I need to share the blame. I thought it would be a great idea if the two of you had rooms next door to each other so you'd see how perfect you are together."

"It's a science, Kenzie," said British. "Any two people can be attracted to each other if they spend time together." It hurt to say the words out loud, especially since she had wanted a temporary fling with him. Why did he have to ruin things by telling her he loved her? And why did she have to go believe him? Why did he have to bring up Christian? It was a low blow and proof that he would say anything to get what he wanted. He wanted to hurt her, so he did.

"Save your science mojo. The point is you two had chemistry together, otherwise nothing would have happened between you." Kenzie wagged her finger in British's face. "And before you want to lie to me, I am the one who cleaned the rooms when Ramon and I returned."

"Oh." British bit her bottom lip and shamefully looked away. She'd been too quick to become intimate with him, physically and emotionally.

Kenzie shoved her hand through her wildly curly red hair. "Anyway, Zoe left here that one time absolutely done with Will."

"And yet they're happily married," British laughed. Laughter was the best medicine. She'd seen the ending to the Ravens show and knew how it ended—that Tracy chick finding a diamond ring in Donovan's dresser drawer. No wonder Donovan didn't want to talk about filming! He'd planned on proposing to the superstar. And could she blame him? Tracy fell perfectly into Donovan's fast-paced world. Meanwhile she was here, just quaint.

"Anyway, Kenzie, look at you, all married now."

"Don't try to change the subject on me," teased Kenzie, frowning. "Why don't you come inside and we can talk? Ramon brought back some of his family's secret-recipe rum."

As tempting as it sounded to sit out back and drink,

British still had to work tomorrow. She needed to think clearly, now that the girls were going to represent South-wood at the next level. "Maybe after the competition? Are you coming to the dance?"

Not only was Kenzie the historian for Southwood, she also taught history at the high school. Every year each of the schools hosted a holiday dance. The teach-ers got a kick out of the parents coming and the students being on their best behavior.

"Ramon and I are chaperoning."

British pushed away from her car to give her friend a hug. "All right, well, we'll catch up soon enough. Tell Mr. Mayor I said good-night and that I voted for him."

"I will," said Kenzie, returning the hug. "He'll be thrilled to know." Earlier in November, Ramon became the first person in over a hundred years to not be born in Southwood to win the mayor's seat.

Before putting her car into gear, British made sure she had the right song selection programmed into her system. She chose a few oldies to take her home—New Edition heartbreakers "Is this the End," "You're Not My Kind of Girl," "Tears on My Pillow," "Can You Stand the Rain," and a few of the solo cuts. Once she had her song choices, she pulled out of the circu-lar driveway. Ramon had joined Kenzie's side and the two waved British off until they disappeared in her rearview mirror.

Heartfelt lyrics belted out of her mouth as British drove down County Road 17. Something about Johnny Gill's deep voice blended with the melodic pitch of Ralph Tresvant's soothed her. She needed to hear it one more time. A light flashed from inside her purse seated in the passenger's seat, exactly where she intended it to stay. British pressed the repeat button on her stereo to sing the song again. She remembered she needed to add Bobby and Whitney's "Something in Common" song. For one brief second British took her eyes off the long dark road. And that was all it took.

Donovan waited on British's stoop until three in the morning. She never arrived. Despite being frozen with the thirty-degree weather, he didn't plan on budging until they spoke. Common sense told him to at least sit in his car with the heated seats on full-blast but he felt he needed this punishment. The list of reasons why he blamed himself. He never should have used Christian against her. He could have worked harder to keep British from walking out on him. British looked past his physical scar and his emotional ones; he should have known better than to scramble and find the one thing to make her hurt before she hurt him. In the end, they both lost.

The last time he looked at her played over in his mind again and again. The hurt look in her chocolate-brown eyes haunted him. He wasn't sure he'd be able to sleep again—which was fine with him. Staying up gave Donovan a chance to watch Southwood settle down. The lights on the giant tree in the town center went off shortly after midnight. The Christmas carousel stopped around the same time. The city went to sleep. So where was British?

Somewhere down the end of the street a garbage truck made its rounds. Just beyond townhome-style businesses, the full moon disappeared and on the opposite side of town threats of yellow streaked the sky.

"Donovan?"

Donovan lifted his head. Maggie and Tiffani from the bakery stopped in front of him. "Hi, ladies."

"Have you been out here all night?" Maggie asked, pushing a white foam cup in his face. The smell of strong coffee wafted through the little hole at the top of the lid.

Nodding, Donovan accepted the cup and mumbled thanks before taking a sip. "Define being out here all night."

Tiffani and Maggie exchanged a look. He'd seen it before. His stomach dropped as he rose. "What happened? Why are you guys here? Where's British?"

"We're here to get a few of her things," Tiffani explained.

"She's staying at her parents', isn't she?" he guessed. Gun or no gun, Donovan fished his car keys out his pocket. He was going to see her tonight.

"Donovan," Maggie said, stepping in his way. "British isn't there. She's in the hospital."

"She was in a car accident earlier tonight," Tiffani provided. "And I'll be damned if it was close to the same spot where Christian wrecked."

"What? Are you serious?" Donovan didn't believe it. "What hospital?"

"Four Points General," said Maggie. "I'll show you. Tiff, you grab her stuff, mmm-kay?"

"'Stuff'?" he repeated. "What happened? How long is British going to be in the hospital? Is she okay?"

Maggie grabbed the keys from his hands and he let her. "I'll drive. I don't think you're in the shape for it."

"Maybe not."

Instead of driving in silence like Donovan hoped, Maggie filled the compartment with idle chatter. She knew Tracy through social networks and did not appreciate the way the starlet had come waltzing into her town. Maggie was actually thinking about making a return to the spotlight just to take it away from Tracy.

Donovan half listened and glanced out the window. Some of the shop owners were getting ready to open. The bread store put out warm smells. The lights over the high school's track flickered on. Life was going on while his stood frozen. He needed to know British was okay. Panic pulsed through to his fingertips. History repeated itself again in the form of a car accident. His. Christian's. And now British's. He needed to see her with his own two eyes.

It didn't dawn on Donovan how fast Maggie drove the Jag. It didn't matter. She got him there and half parked in the lines of the parking space. Inside, the scents of antiseptic and cleanser assaulted his senses. Bright fluorescent lights stung his eyes.

"This way," said Maggie, guiding Donovan through the halls and elevators.

The doors to their floor rang and announced their presence. Donovan found Joan leaning by the window, wrapped in Levi's arms. All of British's siblings were there, as well. His eyes didn't spy any of her in-laws but he figured they were home with the children. Finn and Cree sat across from each other in a set of blue seats with oversize armrests, their legs stretched out on the shared metal coffee table between the two of them. Irish paced the floor and chewed on her fingernails. Scots stood by the nurses' station, tapping his fingers on the desk.

Maggie cleared her throat and announced their presence. "Found someone y'all may know."

"Donovan." Joan pulled away from Levi's embrace and crossed the waiting room. "I'm so glad you're here."

She is? he thought. Either the family hadn't seen the show or they didn't care. Joan hugged him and Cree and Irish came over to greet him, as well. The ladies didn't blame him but the men might. Scots offered a head nod before going back to irritating the nurse with his finger solo. Levi stayed in his spot but considering the bloodshot eyes, Donovan didn't blame him.

"How is she?"

Joan's lips pressed together but still quivered. "She is going to be okay. A bit scarred up, but she's going to be fine."

Absentmindedly, Donovan touched his face. The fifteen-year-old scar ached as bad as his heart. He didn't want her to spend endless nights thinking about the ways to have a scar like his surgically removed. Scar or no scar, Donovan loved her. He understood better than most that beauty was internal.

"Is she awake?"

"We're waiting for the doctors to tell us she is and wants to see anyone."

Cree cleared her throat. "She was conscious when Daddy found her."

"You were there?" Donovan turned his attention to the man dressed in a pair of camouflage overalls.

Half nodding, Levi turned to Donovan. "Yes. I was hunting with some buddies when we heard the crash."

Donovan hated that for him. He wanted to say something comforting but before the words came out, a pixie-haired doctor in teal surgery attire stepped out of a side room. Since everyone rushed to her, Donovan assumed she was the doctor.

"What's going on, Erin?" Scots said, spotting the doctor first. The nurse behind the desk rolled her eyes in relief.

"Dr. Hairston—" Joan slipped from Donovan's side and breezed across the room "—how's British? When can we see her?"

Though he had no right, Donovan stood on the outside of the family, who now surrounded the doctor and plied her with questions. Relief washed over him at the good news. From what he gathered, British's left leg was the point of concern and the concussion had her in and out of consciousness. She has nasty bump on the side of her head and was going to be sore for the next few days and needed to stay in the hospital under observation.

"Can we see her?" Levi asked after the report.

"Family may visit."

A stab of betrayal spurted through him. Donovan rubbed the back of his head. He moved away to give the family some room. Didn't the doctor know British wasn't going to want to be smothered by her siblings, which they more than likely would? Hell, he would, too. Donovan fought against the lump in his throat. He tried to reconcile what the doctor had said and told himself the important point was that British was going to be okay.

The family went in to visit British. Maggie and the woman named Erin started talking and he gathered from their chatter they were related. Of course they were. Everyone in Southwood seemed to be related one way or another.

"Donovan," Levi said at the rear of the group, "you coming?"

The idea of being rejected once again by British didn't sound appealing, especially in front of the Woodburys. "I don't know if she wants to see me."

"Because of your show on television tonight?"

Even with the time alone, Donovan never bothered watching the episode. "I'm not sure what went wrong," Donovan said.

"Did you see it?"

"I was at the STEM-Off," he explained.

Levi motioned for everyone else to go inside while he and Donovan hung back. "It wasn't bad," said Levi, "rather boring, if you ask me."

"Sir, about Tracy…"

"That woman at the end of the show?" Levi shook his head. "I'm the furthest thing from a video producer but it was easy to tell there was nothing between you and her. Hell, half the show on you was the string of women you'd been with."

Donovan hung his head in shame. "I am not that man anymore."

"I know you're not." Levi chuckled. The loving pat on the back Levi gave Donovan made him feel a little bit better about things. Just a smidge. "Donovan, you would have been detected by my kids. I know you care about British and I have no doubt whatsoever she is crazy over you."

As he inhaled deeply, antiseptic scent filled Donovan's lungs. "I'm not too sure about that. A lot has happened in the last six hours."

"Nothing life-altering."

"British was in a car accident." Donovan cocked his head to the side.

Levi lifted his finger. "Almost."

Whether or not the car accident hurt British, harm had come to her and Donovan shouldered the blame. Did she drive while tired? Was she distracted because of him and that's why she wrecked?

"The question is," Levi continued, "what are you going to do about it now?"

"I want to see her."

Levi patted Donovan's back again. "That's what I thought. C'mon."

The door to British's room swept open with a soft

hush. The Woodburys all looked up at Donovan when he entered the room. The heels of his loafers hitting the ground echoed to the beep of the machine monitoring British's heartbeat. His heartbeat. The peaks of the machine perked up when she laid eyes on him. Once again a lump formed in his throat. He barely heard Levi usher everyone else out of the room. He just felt the gust of wind as they left on his face and then again on the back of his neck when the door closed behind him.

A white bandage covered British's long left leg. Another bandage covered the top portion of her head and the middle of her forehead. Donovan closed his eyes. The memory of his accident, from the moment he pumped the brakes one rainy night, came back to him. He touched his cheek and remembered the blood flowing from the open wound on his face. Knowing this had happened to British broke him. He came to her bedside, kneeling automatically. Their hands touched. A plastic monitor clasped down on her index finger. Donovan kissed her fingertips.

"I'm so sorry." He repeated his words over and over, begging her to forgive him.

"This isn't your fault," British said groggily. "You didn't have to come here."

If his body were a cartoon right now, his heart would be shattering. This fight wasn't over. He wasn't leaving. "I love you, British," he professed. "I know you saw a side of me tonight that may have you doubting me. But I'm not that guy I was before. You're everything I never knew I needed in life, British. I need you to understand me. I need you to believe me. I need you to love me."

No matter what anyone told him, he would always feel responsible for this. He pressed his head against the mattress of her bed and did something he hadn't done in a long time. He wept at the realization he could have lost her tonight. He wasn't sure how long he lay like that at her side but after some time, after his knees took the shape of the floor beneath him, British pulled her hand from his, resting it on the top of his head.

"I love you, too."

Chapter 12

Three days in the hospital and a week at home after, British was ready to get back to work. But the doctor insisted on her keeping a light schedule, including not being allowed to attend the Four Points STEM competition.

No matter how much British tried to prove she was fine to walk with a cane, Donovan wasn't hearing it. He made himself at home and in her bed, never allowing her to lift a finger for a thing. If he needed to leave for a few hours, he made sure someone stayed with her and kept her off social media. Donovan hired Dr. Erin Hairston, a former resident of Southwood and sworn childhood enemy of Kenzie's, despite the fact they were first cousins.

With Christmas right around the corner, British began to believe Donovan wasn't going anywhere anytime soon, and she was okay with that. He seemed to enjoy the mundane duties of day-to-day life, including

Christmas tree decorating, which they finally finished last night.

After several arguments of which was better, a multicolorful ornaments and lights tree or one with white lights and matching decorations, British let him take the win. If he loved it, she loved it. The gaudy, overly decorated tree stood in the corner of her living room. Get-well cards and holiday cards mingled on the mantel of the fireplace. Perfectly placed wreaths hung from the four bay windows. And the counters of her kitchen bar were lined with red garlands.

"Well, you have to be excited about tonight," Kenzie said, standing behind British in her bedroom at her tri-mirrored vanity.

Thanks to the same group effort of putting the New Edition posters up on her wall, part of the Tiara Squad had helped to take it down and repaint. She no longer needed to hang on to her past when her future with Donovan was blossoming. Maggie sat on British's cloth-covered new California king bed and pouted. She adjusted the straps of her denim overalls, which were covered in drops of mint and silver paint from this morning.

"What's wrong with you?" British asked, turning her head just enough she didn't mess up the French twist Kenzie attempted to put in her hair.

Maggie shook her head. "I've clearly been in small-town life so long that I am looking forward to living vicariously through you attending a school dance tonight."

Kenzie cursed when she lost the third bobby pin somewhere in British's hair. "Damn it. Explain to me why your boyfriend won't hire a stylist?"

"Something about not trusting anyone with access to the internet." British laughed when she and Kenzie both glanced back over at Maggie.

As if surprised, Maggie's mouth dropped open. "What? I've been disconnected for, like, three months now."

"You should win an award," Kenzie bemoaned with an eye-roll.

"Or at least a man," Maggie mumbled.

A soft knock came at the door. Erin poked her head inside and Kenzie tugged a little tighter on British's hair. "Donovan's here."

Kenzie bent and hugged British by the shoulders. "I don't know if I helped with your hair or not, but either way, you look beautiful."

"If I had my cell phone, I'd take a picture and put you all over Instagram," Maggie agreed. "C'mon, Kenzie, let's sign out and get you ready."

Tonight was going to be British's first outing since her accident. Donovan had refused to let anyone else come over. He'd even made Kenzie and Maggie sign in and out, just in case British got wind of a piece of social media. She thought he was being ridiculous but according to him, she'd find out in due time. She had to trust him. The main thing British wanted to know was how the GRITS team had done.

With a little help from Erin, British came to her feet. In honor of her feeling better, Lexi Pendergrass Reyes sent over a one-of-a-kind perfect dress for British to wear tonight. The bottom half of the dress, made up of soft pink fabric twisted into thousands of roses, covered her white canvas shoes. The off-white sweetheart top was accompanied by a string of pearls around her neck and pearl studs in her ears. The girls exited first.

British took a deep breath, not sure if she was anxious for being able to go out or just from seeing Donovan again. He'd been gone all afternoon and every time he returned home, she greeted him as if he were a soldier coming back from war. She hated being apart from him but looked forward to the deep kisses when he walked through the door.

At first Donovan was seated in the Victorian chair visible from the hallway. He stood and smoothed down the jacket of his black tuxedo. They were attending the middle school dance, both overly dressed, but this was special to her. British set her cane aside by the bedroom door. Donovan closed the gap to meet her.

"I am not sure if I can speak clearly," he whispered in her ear, kissing her on her lobe. British glanced up and found a piece of mistletoe dangling above her door. She responded appropriately with a welcoming kiss and tasted his sweet mouth. He broke the kiss first and dazzled her with a smile that quickened her heartbeat. "I'm tempted to cancel tonight."

"We can at least postpone it," British suggested and tugged his arm back toward the bedroom. "I don't think I can wait until tonight to jump your bones."

"Oh God." The deep groan came from the living room and sounded a lot like Finn.

Sheepishly, Donovan grinned. "I maybe should have started with telling you we weren't alone."

It didn't take a genius for her to guess that her brothers were standing in her living room along with her sisters, parents and her Carres family.

"What are you guys doing here?"

"We're seeing you off to your first dance, dear," said Joan, stepping forward.

Vonna followed and gave British a hug. "We just wanted to see you attend your first dance after so long. We're so happy and glad you're getting better." Her mother-in-law sniffled and allowed Tiffani to pull her to the side.

To humor everyone, British let her family take pictures. Even Will was there and took photos. "I get why your family is here," Donovan whispered as they posed in front of the mantel, "but I don't get why Will has to be here."

"I thought he went back to Miami," British said, "but what would I know? I love how close we've been but you've kept me away from the world."

"I didn't want any distractions. I needed you to heal."

"Donovan, there's no proof that social media distractions hinder body repair."

Donovan turned British around by the hips and dipped his head low for a kiss, making any science, technology, engineering and math leave her mind. Satisfied his kiss left her dumbfounded, Donovan took her by the hand and bid everyone goodbye. For whatever good that did because they all followed them outside, where a man wearing a long-tailed overcoat and top hat stood by a two-horse-drawn carriage. A dark plaid blanket hung on the leather seat for cushion or a breeze.

The weather was perfect for a ride, perhaps a bit cold, but with Donovan's arm around her shoulders she didn't mind.

"This is a bit over the top," British said, "don't you think?"

"I don't know," Donovan said with a shrug. "I've never really done the dating thing. This is how it's done in the movies I watched with my nieces."

The two white horses began to move through the streets of Southwood. "By any chance, were these movies cartoons?"

"Probably. Why? Is this not right?"

British snuggled against his arm. "It's perfect."

People on the streets stopped and waved at them as they rode by. British felt like a princess. It was silly, she knew, but it was fun. They passed city hall and headed down the street toward the middle school but kept going. British gave Donovan a sideways glance. His wink told her not to worry.

Instead of the school's dance traditionally being held in the gymnasium, it was being held at the old beauty school, Mas. Familiar parents' and teachers' cars were parked in the newly paved parking lot.

Zoe met the carriage at the red carpet. Music blared from inside the double doors. She wore a Bluetooth clipped to her ear and had a clipboard propped on her hip. Donovan stepped off first and turned to help British climb down. When she couldn't maneuver with her skirt, he simply lifted her into his arms and set her down in front of his sister-in-law.

"Glad you could make it," Zoe said, giving British a hug. "I haven't seen you since, well, you know."

Donovan followed up the rear and possessively placed his hand on British's lower back when two beefy assistants came to help. "I got this," he told them. "Is everything ready?"

"Five more minutes."

British cocked a look at her date. "What's going on?"

"Let's go in and see."

Inside, the chatter stopped and the live DJ cut the music. The former lunchroom area for the old school had been reconfigured into a winter wonderland. Giant balls of fake snow dangled from the ceiling in a mixture of silver and gold clouds. Her students were so adorable in their formal wear. The young men wore suits and ties and were clean-cut. Her girls all looked like angels. Donovan made everyone back up to give her some room.

Once British finished greeting all the parents and students, Donovan made her sit at the elevated table, where a makeshift Mr. and Mrs. Claus cozy scene was displayed. Instead of the black chairs used at the winter carnival, their chairs were teal and silver, and extremely comfy. She hadn't realized how winded she'd be after saying all her hellos. The GRITS team oddly gathered below and looked to Donovan for approval. Instead of the music cuing back up, a screen lowered from the ceiling.

"Ms. B," Kathleen said, clearing her throat. She held on to a set of note cards. "We wanted to tell you just how much we've missed you since you've been gone."

Natasha stepped forward and started tearing up before she started to speak. Her mother shouted from the back with an encouraging word. Kimber Reyes tiptoed over to hand the girl a tissue. "Okay, whew."

British began to tear up.

"When we thought we'd lost you, we comforted ourselves with the memory of your laughter."

"And filled our playlists with your New Edition music," Lacey interjected.

Stephanie stepped forward. "And while we appreciate everything you've taught us in the STEM world, we also dug back into your old roots when you came back to Southwood to teach home ec."

The girls took a drastic pause and all turned toward Cam Beasley, lurking in the corner by a snowman.

"Anyway," Stephanie said, clicking her tongue against the roof of her mouth. "We know you incorporated science in our daily lives, like making slime with baking soda or how we learned we use physics in roller skating, or even like recycling old cans and turning them into a grill if we're ever lost in the woods, you know, like, teaching impressionable young students how to be self-sufficient."

"And bake peach pies," someone called out.

British craned her neck and was saluted with a plate of pie by Jessilyn. She realized the silver stand between her and Donovan contained a tray of desserts. She made a mental note to taste them later. The lights dimmed.

"So in honor of you," Stephanie said, flicking her braids off her shoulder, "we want to share our STEM challenge for you."

The screen in front came to life with a faux 8 mm film. A New Edition song played in the background as Mrs. Fitzhugh showed up in the hallway of Magnolia Palace the day British arrived. She'd been scared by the girls, which apparently had sparked an idea for them to set up the motion sensor to jingle a set of twinkle lights. The next scene was of a famous rabbit and duck arguing and then tire streaks in the road. A set of numbers counted upward and various signs of deer crossings flashed as the numbers rose. Then the screen went blank. Confused, British glanced over at Donovan. A set of twinkle lights caught her attention and the lights showed a deer in the woods along County Road 17.

"Every time a deer comes close to the country roads where most of them live, it will trigger a set of lights. Sure there are signs that say 'deer crossing' but we never know when, and some of us drive too fast along the roads. So since we cannot predict where or when each deer will cross, the lights will twinkle and signal to the driver that an actual deer is near and he or she can drive with extreme caution," said Stephanie.

"And since the lights are solar," added Natasha, "we won't have to continue changing out batteries."

Mayor-elect Ramon Torres appeared on the screen. "This STEM project is useful and saves lives."

That part garnered a giggle from the girls. "That's my man," Kenzie said dreamily.

When did she get here? British turned in her seat to find her friend. Not only was Kenzie in the back with her husband, so were the rest of the Woodburys.

British's heart started to beat erratically. Her commitment-phobic boyfriend was going to propose. Her hands began to shake. Distracted with thoughts of what kind of dress she'd want and her bridesmaids, she didn't hear the part when Superintendent Herbert Locke appeared on the screen and announced the winner of the Four Points District STEM Challenge. Everyone at the dance exploded with applause.

British did a double take. Forgetting her banged-up leg, she jumped out of her seat to reach the girls, but Kimber flagged her hands back and forth in warning, so she sat back down. "Oh my God," she cried, "you guys! Is this what you've been keeping from me?" She turned to face Donovan and found him sitting there with his hands outstretched, palms facing upward and a rectangular black-velvet box in his hands.

This was it.

The room grew quiet.

British's hands shook. "Is this…?" She paused, worried she'd ruined the surprise for herself by already guessing what he was up to.

"British," Donovan said with a gulp, "I promise I've never been this serious about a life choice and I know I cannot take the next step without you."

Anticipation got the best of her. British bobbed up

and down, then remembered the swelling. She sat down and took the box from his hands. Her polished nails pushed into the lining of the lid and flipped it open.

Hmm, she thought with confusion. Instead of some fabulous diamond she'd expected, she found an old-fashioned silver key. Blinking, she looked into Donovan's smiling eyes and tried to figure out how to get over her disappointment. Instead of asking her to marry him, he was asking her to…shack up?

"This isn't just any key, British," Donovan said softly. "This is the key to the Mas Beauty School. I'm turning part of the building into a satellite office so I can run Ravens Cosmetics and be here with you. I know that with the girls winning the challenge you get more time in the lab at the school but I want you to have your own new fully equipped lab here for experiments for your after-school teams, or you can use it as your own STEM shop if you want."

Her own lab? Any other day she would kill for an opportunity like this, she reminded herself. This was a major step for Donovan, her perpetual bachelor. Keeping that in mind, British palmed the key and opened her arms. "This is wonderful, Donovan."

"So we're doing it?" he asked, pleased as punch.

"We're doing it," British squealed in delight.

Donovan pulled her into his arms. "What I want to do to you is highly inappropriate right now," he whispered in her ear. "But we have prying eyes."

Electricity jolted through her. Everything else was forgotten. "Let's get out of here."

"Perfect."

Everyone seemed to accept the excuse of British being tired. Donovan led her to the horse-drawn carriage again. A car would have been quicker. There was a high probability she and Donovan might do a few naughty things under the heavy plaid blanket.

"So do you promise you like the idea of working together?"

Did it make her a bad person for wanting more this evening? A chance encounter with death had made British realize she wanted Donovan for more than a temporary fling. She loved him with every ounce of breath she had left in her and wanted to spend every moment with him—in matrimony. "I love it. Wait—I can still teach, right?"

Donovan laughed. His arm wrapped around her shoulder felt so natural. "Of course you can. Did I ever tell you about how my grandmother used to work so much that my grandfather, instead of demanding her to stay home more, built a desk next to hers so they could spend more time together?"

"That's so sweet," British cooed. She waved at some of the people on the streets out for an evening walk. Nothing could really get any better than this. She was in a horse-drawn carriage in the town she loved with the man she loved even more. "I'm not sure I can sit next to you all day long, though."

"Don't worry, I wouldn't make you. Besides, I'm not always going to be home."

British sat up. "What?"

"Ravens Cosmetics is based in Miami, so of course I'll have to fly down."

She missed him already. British tried to smile. She fiddled with her bare fingers. "Maybe we can fly together."

"Oh, we're definitely going to travel sooner than later, especially with the holidays in a few days."

Nodding, British understood. The Ravens Cosmetics ad wasn't going to go off like Will had planned. Thanks to taking time away from the company to nurse her back to health, Donovan had never found a replacement model for the job that Tracy girl wanted.

The carriage stopped at the dangling light on Main Street. They were not far from the bakery. British was mad for knowing that. "I'm sorry you never found your perfect girl."

"I found my perfect girl."

"Ha, ha." British wrinkled her nose at him. "You're funny."

"No. Seriously, I found the perfect person for the new line. C'mon and I'll show you. Driver, will you stop here?"

The chauffeur pulled the reins. Donovan got out first then helped British by holding her in his arms again. She half smiled and half bit her lip, knowing she could stay like this forever.

"Look." Donovan pointed to the storefront at Grits and Glam Gowns. The interior lights were off, as expected for a Friday night. The glow of a streetlamp shone on a sprig of mistletoe hanging from the canopy of the doorway. British made a mental note to make him honor the kissing tradition. Donovan snapped his fingers and a set of lights flickered on to shine on a poster-sized advertisement on an easel inside the store. British tiptoed under the awning for a better look. The lavender letters, outlined in gold, gave the name of the product.

"Generations?" British said aloud.

Her eyes focused on the familiar faces staring back at her. Her grandmother, her mom, her sisters and her nieces were all seated together on a long white couch. Their dark hair and beauty popped off the print.

British's eyes roamed quickly, scanning and taking

in every inch of the beauty ad. Everyone was so beautiful. Her heart filled with pride. When her eyes roamed for the third time, she caught a glimpse of the carriage behind her in the oval shape of the window. She spun around to find out where Donovan had gone off to and found him on bended knee.

"British," Donovan said, opening a box. "There's one more thing I needed to ask you this evening."

She was stunned; it took the beating of her heart to get her to realize this was actually it. She opened her mouth and, for the second time since meeting Donovan and looking into his deep, dreamy eyes, she was speechless.

"I've spoken with your father and he has given me permission to take your hand in marriage. Isn't that right, Levi?"

Levi came out of nowhere, probably from right around the corner. "That's right."

Donovan nodded. "I even asked your siblings."

Finn, Cree, Scots, Irish and her sister-in-law Tiffani stepped out next to Levi. "We agree," they chorused.

"And I even asked your moms."

Joan and Vonna appeared. Both ladies were already crying—nodding, but crying just the same.

"So with all this family support, from yours and mine…" Donovan paused for a moment while a group of people she'd only seen on television stepped out of the coffee shop next door. "I am here, on bended knee, asking you to share your life with me. British, will you marry me?"

British was pretty sure she heard New Edition playing somewhere in the background and not just from an MP3 player or CD, but she ignored it and focused on the only thing that mattered—saying yes, which she did, over and over again. Completely forgetting the pain, she dropped to the ground and knelt with him. Both their hands shook as he placed the ring on her finger.

As he placed gentle kisses all over her hands and face. British glanced up and nodded her head at the hanging mistletoe.

"Look, we're following tradition," she said, kissing his chin when he tilted his head upward.

Donovan pulled British into a hug and whispered against her ear, "I love you, babe, and I can't wait to follow more traditions with you while we're creating the next generation together."

* * * * *

KIMANI™
ROMANCE

Soulful and sensual romance featuring multicultural characters.

Look for brand-new Kimani stories
in special 2-in-1 volumes starting March 2019.

Available March 5, 2019

LOVE IN SAN FRANCISCO & UNCONDITIONALLY
by Shirley Hailstock and Janice Sims

A TASTE OF PASSION & AMBITIOUS SEDUCTION
by Chloe Blake and Nana Prah

**PLEASURE AT MIDNIGHT & HIS PICK
FOR PASSION**
by Pamela Yaye and Synithia Williams

**BECAUSE YOU LOVE ME & JOURNEY TO
MY HEART**
by Monica Richardson and Terra Little

Get 4 FREE REWARDS!

We'll send you 2 FREE Books
plus 2 FREE Mystery Gifts.

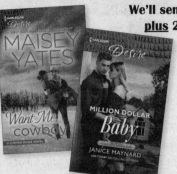

Harlequin® Desire books feature heroes who have it all: wealth, status, incredible good looks... everything but the right woman.

FREE
Value Over
$20

Once she'd heard the rumor about Singleton Financial
wanting to find another firm to represent their conglomeration,
she'd dived for their information. After being trusted to
work with them—although with Leonardo—within the past
year, she felt obligated to encourage them to stay. What had
happened to make them want to leave? It couldn't have been
the work she and Leonardo had done for them; they'd been
happy customers two months ago.

She wouldn't focus on what else had transpired during
that time, but her skin heated at the memory that was trying

to make its way to the forefront of her mind. Soon she'd be face-to-face with the man she'd been avoiding. They'd never been friends, so it hadn't been that hard to stay away. And yet her body still betrayed her on a daily basis and longed for the boar's touch.

Shaking off the biggest mistake of her life, she zoned in on her career. If she could maintain Singleton Financial as a client, she'd definitely be made partner. No way would she allow the muscle-bound Astacio to snatch the chance away from her.

Once again she wondered why he even worked for the firm. His family possessed more money than Oprah Winfrey and Bill Gates combined. He could've gone to work for his family, started his own law firm or even retired. Jealousy roared to life at how easy his life had been.

A buzz from her phone brought her out of her musings just in time to prepare her for the bear who banged her poor door against the wall before storming in. Their erotic encounter hadn't changed him a bit.

Canting her head, she presented a smile sweet enough for him to develop cavities. "How may I help you, Leonardo?" For a rather uptight law firm, they held an open policy about calling people by their first names, although most of the employees called him Mr. Astacio out of terror. She'd rather scrub toilets at an office building again, a job she'd had in high school.

He stopped in front of her desk and braced his hands on it. "You have something that belongs to me."

A thrill shimmied down her spine at being so close to him. Ignoring the way his baritone voice sounded even huskier than normal, she looked around her shared office, glad to find they were alone so they could fight toe-to-toe. "What's that?"

"Don't play games." He pointed to his chest, about to speak again, when an adorable sneeze slipped out. Followed by four more. So the big bad wolf had a cold. From the gossip mill, she knew he never got sick. Detested doing so.

She got to her feet and walked around her desk to the door. She used it as a fan to air the room out. "Since I can't open the windows, I'd prefer if you didn't share your nasty germs with me."

His clenched, broad jaw didn't scare her. Especially considering how his upturned nose now held a tinge of red after blowing it. The man had a monopoly on sexy with his large dark brown eyes and sharp cheekbones. His tailored suit hugged a muscular body she'd jump hurdles to get reacquainted with if he wasn't such an arrogant ass. *And my competition for financial freedom. Mustn't forget that.*

Leonardo held out his hand. "Hand over the file. It's mine."

She'd worn her favorite suit to work, so she had an extra dose of power on her side. Although her outfit wasn't tailored like his, she'd spent more money on the form-flattering dark plum skirt suit than she had on three of her others combined. Kamilla perched a hand on her hip and hitched her upper body forward in a challenge. "Who says?"

"I do."

Tapping her finger against her chin, she shrugged. "Well, that's all the verification I need. I'll give it to you." She sashayed to her desk and sat on the edge. "Right after I'm finished analyzing it."

Don't miss Ambitious Seduction
by Nana Prah, available March 2019
wherever Harlequin® Kimani Romance™
books and ebooks are sold.

KPEXP1218